"Are you okay?"

Shawna gave him a faint nod, as if she wasn't quite certain herself.

He looked closer. As well as the bruising on her throat from the earlier attempt on her life, he noticed the cuts on her knees and hands. "You're hurt," he said.

She turned over her hands and glanced down at her dirty, bloodied palms. "I fell..."

He suppressed a shudder at how close the killer must have come to catching her, to killing her. Whoever the hell it was, he'd gotten too close— too many times. Despite himself, Cole offered the promise she'd sought earlier. "I will protect you," he vowed.

She released a shaky little breath of relief, but then she stared up at him and asked, "Are you sure you want to?"

"It's my job," he reminded her. But she was a hell of a lot more than that to him. She was everything. She had always been...

Everything.

* * *

Be sure to check out the previous books in the exciting Bachelor Bodyguards miniseries.

* * *

If you're on Twitter, tell us what you think of Harlequin Romantic Suspense! #harlequinromsuspense

Dear Reader,

Thank you for picking up the latest installment, *Soldier Bodyguard*, in my Bachelor Bodyguards series! The Payne Protection Agency is at it again—using the family business to protect family. If you've read the previous books in the series and thought matriarch Penny Payne-Lynch was a meddling matchmaker, wait until you meet Cole Bentler's grandfather Xavier Bentler. Grampa X has a couple of reasons for hiring the Payne Protection Agency. One is because he wants to bring his grandson Cole back home to his estranged family and to Cole's high school sweetheart. The second is because someone can't wait for the feisty eighty-six-year-old to die of natural causes.

I modeled Grampa X after my father, who introduces himself to everyone he meets as Grampa Jack. At ninety, he is even more independent and feistier than Xavier Bentler. His car engine never cools off because he goes from restaurant to restaurant meeting up with family and friends—mostly *lady* friends. Like Grampa X, he is independent and determined and also has a heart of gold. I hope you enjoy meeting Grampa X in the pages of *Soldier Bodyguard* and finding out if he can reunite his family, survive the attempts on his life and play matchmaker for Cole.

Happy reading!

Lisa Childs

SOLDIER BODYGUARD

Lisa Childs

HARLEQUIN® ROMANTIC SUSPENSE

Recycling programs
for this product may
not exist in your area.

ISBN-13: 978-1-335-45660-1

Soldier Bodyguard

Printed in U.S.A.

Ever since **Lisa Childs** read her first romance novel (a Harlequin story, of course) at age eleven, all she wanted was to be a romance writer. With over forty novels published with Harlequin, Lisa is living her dream. She is an award-winning, bestselling romance author. Lisa loves to hear from readers, who can contact her on Facebook, through her website, lisachilds.com, or her snail-mail address, PO Box 139, Marne, MI 49435.

Books by Lisa Childs

Harlequin Romantic Suspense

Bachelor Bodyguards

His Christmas Assignment
Bodyguard Daddy
Bodyguard's Baby Surprise
Beauty and the Bodyguard
Nanny Bodyguard
Single Mom's Bodyguard
In the Bodyguard's Arms
Soldier Bodyguard

The Coltons of Red Ridge

Colton's Cinderella Bride

Top Secret Deliveries

The Bounty Hunter's Baby Surprise

The Coltons of Shadow Creek

The Colton Marine

Visit the Author Profile page at Harlequin.com for more titles.

With love and gratitude for my biggest fan and self-appointed publicist, my ninety-year-old dad, Jack Childs aka Grampa Jack. Thank you for promoting my books with everyone you meet and thank you for setting an example in how to live life to the fullest!

Chapter 1

Crazy like a fox. Cooper Payne had never understood that phrase until now. He stared across his desk at Xavier Bentler. This wasn't Cooper's first experience with an interfering grandfather; his wife's guardian/grandfather had been a control freak who had manipulated his granddaughters even from beyond the grave.

"I can't lie to one of my employees," he told the elderly man.

Xavier Bentler was eighty-six years old, but he looked like he was in his sixties. Cooper couldn't believe that he'd had a heart attack a few months ago. Had he really had one? Or just how manipulative was the old man? The heart attack had compelled Cooper's friend and employee, Cole Bentler, to fly *home* for the first time in years—although he hadn't been gone very long.

Was this assignment just another ploy for Xavier to get his grandson Cole home to California again?

"I'm not asking you to lie to him," Xavier said with a cagey grin. "Maybe you can just withhold some information so that he'll accept the job."

Cooper shook his head and ran his hand over his military-short black hair. He was not going to do that again. The last time he'd sent off one of his bodyguards without briefing him fully on the assignment he had nearly lost him—for good. It wasn't a risk he was willing to take again, especially as all the bodyguards who worked for Cooper's franchise of the Payne Protection Agency were his friends and—in the case of Nikki Payne—family.

Hell, after what he'd gone through with his friends, who had all served in the same Marine Corps unit that he had, they were family, too.

"I can't do that," Cooper said. He wouldn't betray a friend…again.

Of course last time it had been more of a joke. But there had been nothing funny about nearly losing Jordan "Manny" Mannes. And this time the danger was even greater.

"You said that a man already died," Cooper reminded the older man.

Xavier Bentler uttered a weary-sounding sigh. "That was most unfortunate. But what's more unfortunate is that his won't be the last death. I am certain that someone else is going to die."

And Cooper was afraid that person would be his

friend if he assigned this job to Cole. He narrowed his eyes as he studied the old man, suspicious of how he could be so certain someone else was going to die. He doubted the guy had what Cooper's mother did— her uncanny ability to just *know* that something was going to happen. Everybody had pretty much envied that ability until now. At least Cooper didn't envy it since he sometimes possessed the ability himself.

Like now…

"Cole can prevent that murder, though," Xavier Bentler continued, "if he protects her."

Cooper had that feeling again—a bad feeling— that he knew who that person was. But still he had to ask, "Shawna?"

The older man nodded and grinned, obviously delighted that Cooper knew who she was. But that was not a good thing. He also knew what she'd already put Cole through. If she died…

Cole would be devastated, no matter what he felt for her yet.

"So you understand," Xavier said, as if he'd successfully argued his case, even though the old guy was a businessman, not a lawyer. "And you will make Cole take this assignment."

Cooper sighed before bobbing his head in a reluctant nod of acquiescence. He did understand that if something happened to Shawna, no matter how badly she'd hurt him, Cole would never forgive himself. Even if Cole didn't want to personally protect her, Cooper had to make sure that nothing happened to her. He just hoped that he wouldn't lose his friend. Either Cole would refuse to take the job and resign from the Payne Protection Agency. Or he would accept the assignment and…

Cole would be the next person to lose his life.

Seeing Shawna Rolfe like this, dressed all in black with tears streaming down her face, was why Cole had ended their engagement. He'd worried that one day she would wind up mourning him like this. Instead she was mourning another man, the one who had become her husband. There was a hollow feeling in Cole's chest as if he'd lost something, as well.

But he had never had it, not for real. If Shawna had ever loved him, she wouldn't have fallen so quickly for someone else. She wouldn't have let another man put a ring on her finger within months of taking off Cole's. And that hadn't been just another engagement ring. It had been the wedding band that she still wore. The yellow gold reflected the sunshine glinting through the stained-glass windows of the church as she lifted her hand to wipe away the tears streaking from beneath her dark glasses. She didn't need the glasses inside the church, so she was probably using them to hide her swollen eyes. But they couldn't hide the fact that she'd been crying and still was.

And that hollowness inside Cole turned to an intense ache. He had never been able to handle Shawna's tears, even when they were just kids in elementary school. He had always beaten up the boys who'd made her cry.

But he couldn't beat up her husband. There was nothing left of him except the ashes in the urn sitting on a podium at the front of the church. There hadn't been much left of him to cremate. A car bomb had blown him to bits.

Why? What reason would anyone have to murder a high school band teacher? Many of those students now played a medley of what they'd claimed had been their beloved teacher's favorite songs. The arrangement was rough as several of them stopped to dissolve into sobs. If Cole believed what he was seeing, then he had to accept that everyone had loved Emery Little. But Cole had grown up knowing how deceptive appearances could be.

Grandfather didn't think the car bomb had been meant for Little. He thought it had been meant for Shawna. It made no more sense to kill a nurse than it did to kill a band teacher. Just a short while ago—as he'd been getting pressed into this assignment—Cole had asked that question. "What reason would anyone have for wanting either of them dead?"

All the Payne Protection bodyguards had been gathered around the conference room table. Cooper had probably called them all in for reinforcements as he'd told Cole what his next assignment would be: protecting his former fiancée.

Thinking it was some sick joke like they sometimes played on each other, Cole had laughed.

But his laughter had evaporated when Cooper had informed him what had happened—and that Cole's grandfather had flown from his estate in northern California out to River City, Michigan, to request their protection services.

"What reason?" Cole had asked again because

none of it made sense. It must have been a horrible mistake. "What's the murderer's motive?"

"Jealousy," Nikki Payne had offered, and her auburn brows had arched over her brown eyes as she'd studied him.

He was the only one who would have a reason to be jealous. But maybe Lars Ecklund, Nikki's fiancé and Cole's friend, hadn't shared his history with her. So Cole told her, "I broke my engagement to Shawna a long time ago."

They had been engaged a long time as well—first with the promise ring he'd given her when they'd graduated high school and then with the engagement ring he'd given her when he'd returned from boot camp. When he'd broken up with her six years ago, before his unit's most dangerous mission, Shawna had tried to give back the engagement ring—a two-karat solitaire he'd bought after he'd inherited his father's estate. But he hadn't wanted it back. He hadn't even thought he'd make it back from that mission. But he had—to find her already married to another man.

"I have no reason to be jealous," he'd insisted.

But he was.

As he stood there and watched Shawna weep over another man, jealousy churned his stomach into an acidic pool of bile. No. Everyone hadn't loved Emery Little. He hated the man, for making Shawna cry. Most of all he hated him for making Shawna love him, the way she hadn't really loved Cole.

He shouldn't have lied in that meeting—because his boss had used that lie against him. "If you have no reason for jealousy, then you have no reason to refuse this assignment," Cooper had pointed out. "You better file a flight manifest. You need to fly out right away so you don't miss the funeral."

Now he wished like hell that he had. He couldn't stand it. He couldn't bear listening to everyone sing praises about Shawna's husband while she wept over him. At least he wasn't suffering alone. When Cooper had turned the tables on him, Cole had spun it back around on all of his friends.

"I'll take it on one condition," he'd said.

Much like his little sister, Cooper had arched one of his dark brows. Maybe he'd been silently reprimanding an employee for placing conditions on a job or maybe he'd just wanted to know what that condition was.

"You all work this assignment with me." Maybe Cole had been counting on Cooper refusing because he'd never wanted his friends to know much about his old life. And he'd certainly never intended to show it to them.

"That doesn't sound like the best use of Payne Protection resources," Cooper had said.

And Cole had snorted. "Hasn't the past taught us we're the safest and the most efficient when we all work together?"

Cooper hadn't been able to argue that. So they all stood in the pew with him: Cooper, Manny, Dane, Lars and Nikki. His grandfather hadn't hired just one bodyguard; he'd hired all of Payne Protection. At least, all of Cooper's franchise. There were still two others, run by Cooper's brothers, Logan and Parker.

All of Cole's coworkers and friends were here, so

he wasn't alone. And he sure as hell wasn't the only one suffering. Not at this funeral…

Finally, it ended with Shawna filing out of that front pew to take her husband's ashes. Still so slender and petite, she looked too delicate to lift the heavy urn, but she handled it easily if reluctantly. She still wore her hair long, the silky black tresses skimming down her back nearly to her thin waist. It flowed as she turned away from the front of the church. But she paused again at that first pew before starting down the aisle. And a little girl stepped out to take her hand.

Cole's breath left his lungs. She had a child. He had no doubt the little girl was Shawna's. With her long, silky black hair and pale skin, she looked exactly like Shawna had when he'd met her so many years ago on the elementary school playground, tears streaming down her face because some bully had knocked her down and she'd skinned her knees. This little girl's knees weren't skinned, but she was crying, her heart broken over the loss of her father.

Of course Cole should not have been shocked to see the child. He'd heard Shawna and her husband had started a family. That was why his visit home when his grandfather had his heart attack had been so brief. He hadn't wanted to risk running into Shawna then.

He should have refused this assignment. But how?

He'd loved Shawna too much to risk her getting hurt—even because of him. So he couldn't let anyone else hurt her either. What if the bomb had been meant for her? What if the person tried again and killed Shawna or her child?

He couldn't risk it—just like his grandfather. The cagey old bastard had known. Xavier Bentler stepped out of the pew behind the little girl and started down the aisle with the child and her mother. Shawna was his nurse; she was supposed to be taking care of him. But it appeared to be the other way around, at least at the moment.

They continued down the aisle toward the pew in the back that Cole and his friends had slipped into when they'd arrived a few minutes late. Shawna was looking down, one arm wrapped around that urn while her other arm was stretched out, her fingers linked with her daughter's small ones. He didn't expect her to notice him.

But just as she neared the pew, she glanced up and even through her dark glasses, their eyes met and held. She paused for a moment—until the little girl tugged her forward and Cole's grandfather put his hand on her back. Over her head, Xavier met Cole's gaze and nodded. Then he guided Shawna out of the church to the long black car waiting at the bottom of the church steps.

They had already inspected that vehicle, making certain no explosive devices had been planted on it. But still Dane slipped out of the other side of the pew and down the stairs to join the driver in the front seat. Astin, the chauffeur, had worked for Grandfather for years. He could handle the driving, but he didn't have the gun Dane carried.

Cole hoped Dane didn't have to use it, not with the

child in the car. At least the trip would be a short, and hopefully uneventful, one.

Even before the minister announced that Xavier Bentler had invited everyone back to his home for a memorial luncheon, Cole knew that was where he would be heading next. Home. Not that the monstrous mansion had ever really felt like home.

Cole glanced at his friends. Manny wouldn't be surprised; he knew more than the others did about Cole's life. But now everyone would know exactly how damn rich he was—so rich it was embarrassing. That was one of the reasons why he hated talking about himself or the past. But that wasn't the only reason. It hurt too damn much when he thought of it because he always thought of *her*.

He was home.

And Cole Bentler looked even more handsome than he did every time she'd thought of him over the past six years. His hair was dark gold and his eyes such a deep blue. He seemed taller than she remembered him and much more muscular, but then some of her memories were of the boy Cole had been, not of the man he had become.

Just as she'd been warned, he had changed after joining the Marines. Not after boot camp. After boot camp, he'd come home and proposed to her. It was after all the missions, after leaving for months on end, that he had returned tense and distant and different.

It was easier to remember the sweet, sensitive boy with whom she'd fallen in love than the cold, unemotional man who'd broken her heart.

What in the world was he doing here? As Shawna settled into the back seat of the limousine and Xavier Bentler sat across from her, head down as if unwilling to meet her gaze, she knew. "You told him?"

That was where Xavier had gone. Some time yesterday, he had slipped away for several long hours. She hadn't been too concerned at the time. She'd figured he'd sneaked away to play a round of golf and smoke the cigars she'd banned from the house. She should have known Cole's grandfather had been up to something; he usually was.

And as usual he was completely unabashed at getting caught. He nodded.

But she was still surprised that Cole had showed up. Even after he'd heard about her husband's funeral, she doubted he'd have any compulsion to attend it.

"I hired him to be your bodyguard," he added.

And she gasped.

So did Maisy. "Why does Mommy need a bodyguard?" Then her blue eyes widened in realization and fear. "So nobody kills you like they killed..." Her voice cracked with sobs.

Shawna slid across the seat and wrapped her free arm around the child's thin shoulders. Her heart broke every time she heard her daughter cry and saw her fear. Shawna had done her best to try to shield the five-year-old from all the news broadcasts. But even if Maisy hadn't heard it from the media, she would have known about the car bomb. The explosion had woken her up.

Fighting to keep her voice calm and steady, she

told Xavier, "I don't need a bodyguard." She glared at him, hoping he would take the hint.

"Yes, you do!" But it was Maisy who argued with her. "You need to make sure nobody tries to kill you, too!"

Shawna's heart broke again at the terror in the child's voice. She pulled her daughter closer and held her trembling body. "You don't have to worry about that," she assured her. "Nothing's going to happen to me."

Maisy's head bobbed up and down in a quick nod. "I know," she agreed. She fluttered her long black lashes and stared up at her with those deep blue eyes of hers and added, "Because Grampa X hired you a bodyguard."

But the man he'd hired to protect her was the one who'd already hurt her more than anyone else ever had. Who would protect her from him?

Especially if he ever learned the truth...

Chapter 2

How could he protect someone when he couldn't be in the same room with her? That wasn't completely Cole's fault, though. Shawna had yet to remain in any one area. Maybe it was just that she was moving from guest to guest, speaking softly with everyone as she accepted their condolences and expressed her own to them.

Or maybe, as he strongly suspected, she was trying to avoid him—because every time he entered a room, she left it.

And there were a lot of rooms in his grandfather's house, so many that Cole had been able to do his best to avoid his family. They were all here, all still living in the French provincial mansion. Even his mother lived here with his stepfather. And of course his two uncles and their assorted offspring would never venture out on their own.

But he had had no idea how entwined their lives were with Shawna's yet. He had broken up with her nearly six years ago, yet she seemed more a part of his family than he had ever been.

Of course that had been different when his father was alive. Then Cole had felt as if he'd belonged— at least with his father. Coleman Bentler Sr. had not lived here. Nor had he worked for Xavier, like his older brothers did. He'd made his own money and his own way in the world.

But when Dad had died…

To Cole, he had bequeathed all of his money and his family's resentment. Cole could understand why his mother would have been angry. Tiffani and his father had never been happily married. In fact, she'd admitted to purposely getting pregnant to trap him into marriage. In the end, Coleman had gotten his revenge when he'd cut her out of his will along with a lot of other relatives who for some reason thought they were entitled to inherit.

No, these people who glared at Cole with such hatred and anger were not his family.

His unit was his true family. He'd been a fool to worry about what they'd think of his wealth. When they'd seen the house, not one of them had made a comment or even blinked in surprise. Money didn't matter to this family of his. Manny, Cooper, Lars and Dane were like his brothers. The rest of the unit, the ones who were still enlisted, they were his extended family—the ones he didn't get to see all that often but who were forever in his heart and thoughts.

Shawna had been forever in his heart and thoughts. He'd loved her so much that he had never wanted anything but happiness for her, even at the expense of his own. Had she been happy with Emery?

The guy had called him once and wanted to talk to Cole. But he had been about to leave for another mission and hadn't had the time or the inclination. Nor would he have been able to handle the distraction. The last thing he'd wanted to do was have a discussion with the man sleeping with the woman Cole had loved. He couldn't remember exactly what he'd said to the guy to get rid of him, but it probably hadn't been too nice.

He felt a pang of regret now as he approached the urn. It had been set up on a table in the library, flanked with flowers and photos of the dark-haired, dark-eyed man. Emery Little had been a good-looking guy—the kind of guy who was so good-looking he was almost pretty. Or maybe that was just more of Cole's jealousy seeping out.

"Did you know my daddy?" a soft voice asked, and small fingers grasped his arm, tugging on it to draw his attention.

As Cole looked down at the little girl, he felt another pang. But he couldn't identify it. Was it regret that she wasn't his child? Jealousy that she was another man's? Or was it just that she reminded him so damn much of her mother?

She looked so much like Shawna, just like a little doll, with her mother's black, silky hair and porcelain skin. She didn't have Shawna's warm brown eyes, though. The child's were a deep, bright blue.

"Did you know Daddy?" she asked again as she stared up at him.

He shook his head. "No. I knew your mother…" Or at least he'd thought he had. But he'd been wrong, painfully wrong.

Her eyes brightened with recognition, and she exclaimed, "I know who you are!"

Had Shawna showed her daughter his photo before? She would have had enough of them—from every prom and homecoming dance they'd attended— along with all the candid pictures she used to take of him. Or had she destroyed all of those when he'd ended their engagement?

The little girl answered his unspoken question when she exclaimed, "You're Grampa X's grandson!"

His grandfather had photos of him around the house. At graduation, in his uniform.

But then he tensed as he realized what she'd called his grandfather. "Grampa X?"

Why would she refer to him as that?

Could she be…

Cole's heart slammed against his ribs as the thought occurred to him. Could she be *his*?

Shawna had been so busy avoiding Cole that she'd lost track of her daughter. There were so many people in Xavier's home—so many mourners. Emery had been a wonderful man, sweet and caring. He hadn't deserved to die like he had. But then nobody did.

He had only been gone a couple of days, and she

already missed him—so much. And so did Maisy. But Shawna didn't miss Emery like she'd missed Cole. While she'd loved Emery, she'd never been in love with him.

He hadn't cared, though. He hadn't been in love with her either. They had only been very good friends. And because neither had been able to spend their lives with the one they really loved, they had decided to build a life together—for Shawna's baby.

Maisy…

Where had she gone?

Had all the sympathy and tears gotten to be too much for her? It had for Shawna.

She felt like a hypocrite. Everyone thought she and Emery had had the perfect marriage. But they hadn't had a real marriage at all.

But maybe that was what had made it perfect. They hadn't had to deal with the mess of real love— with the passion, with the insecurity and hurt.

After Cole, Shawna had vowed to never again risk that kind of pain. And she'd vowed to be Emery's wife. She'd never expected him to leave her like this.

She had thought that maybe someday he would leave her to finally be with the person he really loved. She had wished him that happiness, and for the past few days, he'd seemed hopeful that it might finally be possible.

Was that person here among the other mourners? Shawna had no idea who it was. Emery had never told her the name of his beloved. Maisy might know, though. She was the epitome of little pitchers having big ears; the child never missed a bit of gossip.

Unfortunately...

Was she hiding somewhere now, eavesdropping on conversations? Or had she gone to the library to find solace in her books?

Shawna slipped through a group of mourners in the hall, passing them with nods but not letting them stop her. She had a sudden instinct that she needed to find Maisy. Now. She quickened her step and rushed through the open pocket doors into the library. And a gasp slipped through her lips when she found Maisy—talking to her father.

Cole stared down at the little girl, and Shawna could see the speculation on his face. He was wondering...

If he realized...

He would hate her even more than Shawna hated him.

"Hey, Maisy," she called out to her daughter. "You know what I've told you about talking to strangers."

Maisy laughed as if Shawna were joking. Had the little girl figured it out? Or had she overheard the speculation about her paternity that had been rampant ever since Shawna had started showing. Fortunately it had taken a while for her pregnancy to show. Or it wouldn't have been just speculation.

"Cole isn't a stranger, Mommy," Maisy protested. "He's Grampa X's grandson."

Cole turned toward Shawna and arched one of his dark blond brows. "Grampa?"

"He insists she call him that," Shawna said, "since we've been staying with him." Actually he'd insisted on it even before that. She suspected he knew the truth, although he'd never outright asked her.

"You live here?" Cole asked, his jaw dropping in shock.

"I work for your grandfather," she said. She hadn't intended to quit her job at the hospital, but Xavier hadn't had to do much to talk her into it. She'd been devastated when he'd come into the ER while she was working. He'd been so close to death.

She had already lost so many people she cared about. She had vowed to do whatever she could to keep Xavier alive. But that had meant quitting her job at the ER. She'd even had to scale back on the hours she spent at the high school as assistant coach to the cheerleading squad. And that was a job she'd done since she'd been in high school herself. That was the job that had brought about her friendship with Emery.

Had nobody told Cole that she was working for his grandfather now? But then he rarely had anything to do with his family. She could understand his reasons regarding the rest of them.

But his grandfather…

And his mom?

She could not understand Cole cutting the two of them out of his life. She would do anything to have her family back again. But her parents had died, in a tragic accident on one of their weekly date nights, when she was so young that she sometimes struggled to remember them. Would Maisy remember Emery?

He had been so good to the little girl. He'd treated her like she was his. He could not have loved her any more had she been. Shawna hadn't had that experience with her aunt and her cousins when she'd come to live with them. If it hadn't been for Cole...

She would have felt so alone. But the first day of elementary school, Cole had beat up her cousin for her and had threatened he would hurt the kid worse if he ever picked on her again. Cole had been her hero back then.

Now he was her nightmare.

"I work for Grandfather now, too," Cole said.

Her stomach twisted into knots at the reminder. "He shouldn't have hired you," she said. "I have no need for a bodyguard."

"Yes, you do!" Maisy said. "I don't want anything to happen to you!" And she burst into tears, her thin shoulders shaking with her desperate sobs.

Shawna knelt to pull the little girl into her arms. But Cole was already there, lifting up the child. The move shocked both mother and daughter, so much that Maisy immediately quieted.

While he held her on one of his mammoth arms, he tipped up her chin with his other hand. "I won't let anything happen to your mother."

Maisy blinked her thick black lashes and stared up at him with eyes that mirrored his. And panic clutched Shawna. How could he not know? How could he not stare into those eyes and immediately recognize that the little girl was his?

Maisy tilted her head as she studied his face. Did she see it, too? Or was she trying to determine whether or not to believe him? "Really?" she asked.

He nodded. "Yes, really," he assured her. "I'm a bodyguard. That's what I do—I protect people."

A shaky little sigh slipped through Maisy's rosebud lips. "I wished you would've protected Daddy."

"I didn't know he was in danger," Cole told her. "Or I would've."

And now he'd lied to their child twice—first when he'd promised to protect Shawna and now when he'd claimed he would have protected Emery. She was aware that her friend had tried to reach out to him. A hopeless romantic, Emery had wanted to help Shawna find her happy ending, even though at that time he'd given up on ever having his own. After that conversation with Cole, he'd given up on hers, as well.

"Emery wasn't in danger," Shawna said defensively. "What happened was just a horrible accident."

"It was a bomb," Maisy said, her little voice quavering.

Shawna flinched. Her little spy needed to stop eavesdropping on adult conversations. Unfortunately, she'd had a front row seat to the explosion.

Cole turned toward her and arched a dark blond brow again. He was surprised, too, that the child knew so much. But before Shawna could explain, Maisy added, "I heard it 'splode. It broke my window."

The blast had broken several windows in the cute little bungalow while rattling the rest of them.

"It happened here?" Cole asked.

Shawna shook her head. "Our home."

She had been there, packing up more of their stuff to move to the Bentler estate. Maisy had spent the night there—with Emery, who'd still been living in their house. He'd just been leaving for work.

"Grampa X says this is our home now," Maisy said. "That he needs us to live here, to take care of 'im."

Shawna suppressed a derisive snort. Sure, Xavier had had a heart attack. He had health issues. But he was the one taking care of them—especially now.

"Why don't you go check on Grampa?" Shawna suggested. "Make sure he's okay."

The little girl nodded and wriggled down from Cole's arms. He released her quickly, almost as if he was surprised to find himself holding her. Apparently his instinct to comfort and protect hadn't completely deserted him. Maybe he'd lost it only that day he'd broken their engagement and Shawna's heart. He hadn't comforted and protected her then. He'd just walked away.

Maisy hadn't walked away yet. Despite wriggling out of his arms, she caught his hand and tugged on it until he hunched over so they were face to face. Then she lifted her other hand to his cheek and stared into his eyes.

She was such an observant little girl, which unnerved Shawna for so many reasons. How would she feel if she learned the truth? Would she hate Shawna for lying to her?

"You promise you will protect my mommy?" the little girl asked the bodyguard.

Cole stared at her for several long seconds before solemnly nodding and replying, "I promise."

His word was good enough for the little girl who dropped her hand from his face and scampered out of the library.

Still crouched down, Cole released an unsteady

breath. And panic stole Shawna's breath away entirely. He'd noticed. He suspected...

"She's quite precocious," he remarked. Then he straightened up and looked down at Shawna, his blue eyes intense. "How old is she?"

She knew what he was asking. What he wanted to know...

Unlike him, she couldn't outright lie like he had to their daughter. "Five," she said, then forced herself to add the word that would mislead him. "Just five."

Implying that she'd just had a birthday, which would have made her too young to be his daughter. But Maisy hadn't just had a birthday. That special day was actually coming up soon. In just a couple of weeks, she would be six. He couldn't be here for her birthday, or he would know what the rest of his family only suspected.

She'd tried to convince them that Maisy had been premature. Since she was so tiny, they had believed her even though she'd actually been two weeks late. But then they'd probably wanted to believe her. They wouldn't want Maisy to be another possible heir they would have to battle. They constantly bickered with each other—over their allowances from their grandfather and over the money they would eventually inherit from him.

That was another reason why Shawna had agreed to become Xavier's private nurse. She wanted him to live forever, both because she loved the old man and to spite his spiteful family. They'd never treated Cole well either, especially after he'd been made the sole heir of his father's estate.

Not that she cared about Cole anymore.

She loved Xavier, though. He had always been so good to her. All those times Cole had left her for boot camp and for those long deployments, they had bonded together over their concern for him. Even after Cole had broken up with her, she'd still been there for Xavier, offering him comfort and hope, while he worried about his favorite grandchild.

Shawna couldn't entirely meet Cole's blue-eyed gaze, but she could feel him staring at her. Goose bumps of awareness and fear rose on her skin. She shivered a little.

"She's sweet," he said. "Looks just like you did."

"My mini-me," she said. "That's what Emery always called her." Her voice cracked as she thought of her dear friend. More tears threatened despite the fact that she should have already been completely dried out. She blinked them back.

"I'm sorry for your loss," he said.

It was a loss. But it wasn't her first one. Not by far.

First she'd lost her parents. And then she had lost the love of her life: Cole. She would not feel sorry for herself, though, not when she had so many other blessings.

Like Maisy…

Emery was the one who had lost everything—his life.

"I don't understand it," she mused. "I don't understand why anyone would want to harm Emery."

"I read the police report," Cole said. "The bomb wasn't in his car. It was in yours. The bomb was meant for you."

Shawna gasped, feeling as though she'd been punched. Of course it had been her car. She hadn't been using it since she'd started working for Xavier. He always insisted that she use his car and driver. So when Emery's vehicle hadn't started that morning, she'd suggested he use hers. She'd urged him to take it and keep it.

The little SUV had just been sitting in the garage for weeks. She'd teased him about letting the newer vehicle sit while he continued to drive his clunker. But because theirs had never been a real marriage, Emery had always been hesitant about using anything of hers. He had been hesitant that morning, too.

If only she hadn't pushed him. She should have had him use Xavier's car and driver instead. But then she and Maisy might have gotten into hers.

She didn't care about her own life. But Maisy was just a child. She had her entire life ahead of her.

The tears rushed over Shawna again, and she couldn't fight them this time. Sobs racked her body, making her tremble. Then strong arms wound around her, drawing her against a hard, muscular body. And she began to tremble even harder as fear overwhelmed her.

Now she wasn't just afraid for Maisy but she was also afraid for her heart. It was reacting to Cole's closeness. It was pounding fast and furiously, and beneath her cheek, she could feel his heart pounding just as fast and furiously.

No. He could not be her bodyguard because no matter what promise he'd made their daughter, he would not be able to protect her.

Even if that bomb had been meant for her, like he'd claimed, he still posed the greater threat to her. She still reacted to him, just as she had when she'd loved him. And she could not fall for him again.

Loving him last time had nearly destroyed her. If she fell for him again, she was terrified she might not survive.

Xavier Bentler smiled as he softly slid the pocket door closed on the couple embracing inside the library. He didn't want anyone to interrupt them. Not even their daughter. When Maisy had caught him standing in the hallway, he'd sent her off to the kitchen to get him some cookies. Fortunately Shawna hadn't banned them from the house like she had his cigars.

He turned away from the door and slammed into what felt like a steel post. Cooper Payne steadied him with a strong hand on his shoulder.

"You're playing a dangerous game," the younger man warned him.

"What game?" Xavier asked, feigning innocence.

"My mother's a wedding planner," Cooper related. "I know a matchmaker when I see one."

Xavier shrugged. "I have no idea what you're talking about. My nurse is obviously in danger. She needs protection." He had a bad feeling that she could be in danger because of him.

"And you could have hired any other security firm besides ours," Cooper said. "You could have even hired one of my brother's franchises of the Payne Protection Agency. But you chose mine. No." He pointed toward the closed pocket doors. "You chose *him*."

Unabashed, Xavier nodded in agreement. "Of course I did. He's my grandson. I know he's the best."

And he also knew nobody would protect Shawna like Cole would. Xavier was pretty damn sure that was why the stubborn young fool had broken their engagement all those years ago. Cole had been trying to protect Shawna from the pain of losing him.

Damn fool. He'd just put her through that pain sooner.

His grandson's boss studied him through narrowed blue eyes. The guy was shrewd. Xavier understood why he was friends with Cole.

"He's good," Cooper acknowledged. "All my guys—and my sister—are very good. They will do everything within their power to keep Shawna and her daughter safe."

"Good," Xavier said as he released a breath of relief. "That's what I hired you to do."

Cooper snorted. "We both know that's not the only reason you hired us. You're playing matchmaker. And that's a dangerous game."

"More dangerous than bombs?"

"When emotions are involved, things get messy," Cooper warned. "People get distracted. Cole can't afford to be distracted right now. You hiring him has put him in even more danger than she is—in even more danger than he was on our missions for the Marine Corps."

Xavier tensed as fear replaced his earlier satisfaction. "How's that?"

"Because Cole will give up his life for hers," Cooper said.

"But you're all here," Xavier said. "You'll all work together to keep her safe."

"Her," Cooper said. "But Cole's going to be more worried about protecting her and that child than himself. He's now in more danger than she is."

Xavier hadn't considered that. He'd known his grandson had defied odds before—in the Marines, even in his new role as bodyguard. But he hadn't considered that the job he had hired him to do could be the one that would get him killed.

What the hell had he done?

Chapter 3

His heart beating frantically, Cole hadn't been this afraid…since the last time he'd held Shawna Rolfe in his arms. But she wasn't Shawna Rolfe anymore. She was Shawna Little. She was another man's wife.

But having her in his arms again felt so right, felt so natural. She fit just as perfectly as she always had even though she was so petite and he was tall. She was delicate, and he was tough. Actually they had never really fit at all.

He should have never proposed to her in the first place, not when he'd been leaving for the Marines. He'd been young and arrogant then and so convinced that he was invincible. After his father's death, he should have known no one was, if his incredibly strong, independent father was not.

But it had taken a few deployments for him to understand how tentative his life was. And he hadn't wanted to put her through yet another loss. Her parents' deaths had nearly destroyed her.

But losing him hadn't affected her at all. She'd moved on quickly. And really, he had tried to be happy that she'd had. That she had a husband with a good, safe job. Emery Little shouldn't have died.

So Cole offered his condolences again with all sincerity. "I'm sorry."

Shawna pulled back, tugging free of his arms. "Why?" she asked.

"Your husband died."

Her usually pale skin flushed. "I know. But why are you sorry about that?"

"I didn't want him dead," Cole said. "Hell, that was the last thing I wanted."

She flinched.

"Because I wanted you to be happy," he explained.

"Why?" she asked the question again, her brow furrowing with confusion. "When you broke up with me…"

He'd had to say terrible things to get her to accept that they were over, that she had no reason to wait for him. Obviously he'd gotten through to her far too well.

"We were not meant to be together," he said. Then or now. His life as a bodyguard was no less dangerous than his life had been as a Marine. "But that didn't mean I didn't want you to be happy."

He would have preferred that she had waited a little longer though before she'd married someone else and started a family with him. But then he was a hypocrite because the whole reason he'd broken up with her was so she wouldn't mourn him. Mission accomplished.

She shook her head in denial. Obviously she didn't believe him. He wasn't going to argue with her- not while she was in mourning.

"Why are you here, Cole?" she asked.

"My grandfather hired the Payne Protection Agency to protect you."

"Why are *you* here?" she asked.

"My boss assigned me to this job."

She chuckled bitterly. "And what—he would fire you if you refused the assignment?"

"Maybe." But he doubted it. Cooper probably would have understood if Cole had told the truth, that he was not over her, that he would never be completely over her. But Cole had lied, had claimed that he had no reason to be jealous of her and her dead husband. Why the hell had he lied?

"And what if he had fired you?" she challenged him. "You could start your own damn security firm. Or you could never work another day in your life like the rest of your family."

While they were all employed at his grandfather's billion-dollar business, it was a joke. None of them actually did any real work.

And that was why Cole worked. He didn't want to be like the rest of his family. She knew that because she'd once known him better than anyone else ever had. Or so he'd thought.

Maybe she'd married another man because she

had known how much it would hurt him. And she'd wanted to hurt him like he had hurt her.

"My family is the Payne Protection Agency," he said. "I served with them." On the battlefield and on the bodyguard frontlines. He wasn't talking just about his former unit but about Nikki and the rest of the Payne family who'd embraced him and his friends like their own.

"So that's why you didn't say no?" she asked. "Because you couldn't let *them* down?"

He heard the bitterness and resentment in her voice. Did she still hate him for breaking up with her? Even after all these years, even after she'd found happiness with another man? Of course that happiness was over now.

Emery Little was dead.

And Cole needed to find out why. Had the killer really intended Shawna as the target? If so, she was in serious danger. "You need a bodyguard," he pointed out. "Even your daughter is worried about you."

"I'm okay with having a bodyguard," she said. "To make Maisy feel more secure. But I don't want that bodyguard to be you."

"Why not?" he asked.

"You know why," she said.

But he shook his head. "You got married. You had a kid. You moved on."

"But I never got over…"

His heart flipped in his chest. Had she never gotten over him—just as he had never really gotten over her?

"…what you said," she finished. "When you broke up with me, you told me that you couldn't play hero anymore to my damsel in distress. That there were people in real danger who needed you."

He barely remembered what he'd told her then. He'd just needed to make her mad enough to agree to the breakup. Again, mission accomplished.

"You told me that I had to grow up and finally learn to take care of myself for once." Her face was flushed now and her eyes were bright with anger.

Cole's own temper flared now. "And instead of listening to me, you married some other guy within weeks of our breakup, so that he could take care of you!"

"You son of a bitch!" she cursed him.

He'd been called that before—by his own father. Coleman hadn't been insulting him, though. He'd been insulting his wife. Cole's parents had hated each other that much. That was another reason Cole never should have proposed to Shawna. He had no idea how to have a successful marriage. His parents' had been a disaster. And none of his grandfather's three marriages had lasted. His uncles had certainly not set good examples for him either.

He didn't argue with Shawna's assessment of him. He couldn't.

She turned and ran toward the doors—that at some point somebody must have closed. She fumbled with them before cursing again and sliding them open just wide enough for her to slip out into the hall.

Cole shouldn't have said what he had—six years ago or now.

Especially not now.

She had just lost her husband in what had probably

been an attempt on her life. Her life was in danger. Remembering that no matter what she said he was supposed to be protecting her, he rushed toward the doors. He pushed them open the rest of the way and stumbled out into the hall.

But she was gone.

Where had she gone?

Shawna dragged in a deep breath as she stepped outside. The sweet, acrid scent of cigars filled her lungs, making her cough and sputter. She found the butt of a cigar, the tip still glowing, lying beside the steps leading out the back door of the garage.

So this was where Xavier came to smoke. Of course if she confronted him, the old codger would probably blame the chauffeur. And Astin, being as loyal as he was, would willingly cover for him.

Xavier charmed everyone—even her—into doing what he wanted. That was why Cole was here. It wasn't because he cared about her; he'd made his opinion of her abundantly clear six years ago and again just now in the library.

She wasn't the helpless female he had accused her of being, though. She hadn't married Emery to protect her. She'd married Emery to protect Maisy. She hadn't wanted anyone to know her child was a Bentler, hadn't wanted to subject a baby to the resentment and anger Cole had endured.

And because she wanted to protect Maisy, Shawna would agree to have a bodyguard. Anyone but Cole, though. Her superhero when they were kids. And as a Marine, decorated for his heroism, he had also been a superhero. Why had he changed with her?

Why had he become as cruel as the people from whom he'd once protected her when they were kids? What had she done to him?

Sure, she'd married Emery, but that had been only after he'd broken their engagement and her heart. She never would have stopped loving him, if he hadn't stopped loving her first.

He still affected her. Even after all these years— even after how much he'd hurt her, he still affected her physically. Emotionally. Passionately.

She wanted to feel nothing. She wanted to be numb—like she had been when she'd gone into shock after the explosion, after she'd realized what had happened to Emery.

Poor Emery.

She blinked back tears. She needed to get back inside, back to mourning her husband and best friend. But she didn't want to see Cole again. She doubted he had left despite being told she didn't want him as her bodyguard. But it wouldn't matter even if he had left. She would still see him—as she saw him all the time—in her mind.

Sometimes he was the boy who'd rescued her and protected her. Sometimes he was the man who'd taught her about love and passion. And sometimes he was the monster who'd broken her heart.

She tensed as she thought of him, but it wasn't with just anger. She realized that in her haste to get away from him she had stepped outside alone. If she was in real danger, that wasn't the smartest idea.

And while she would rather not believe that bomb had been meant for her, it had been in her car. Not Emery's...

She shivered now as a cold chill raised goose bumps along her skin. Her black dress had long sleeves, but it was lightweight material. She needed a sweater. Hell, she needed to be back inside—with people.

With Maisy...

Pushing open the service door, she stepped back into the garage. The lights that had been on moments ago were off. Had she accidentally flipped them off as she'd walked out? But when she touched the switches, she found them facing up already. Turning them the other way didn't do anything.

Had the power gone out?

There was no storm raging outside. That was only inside her—in her head and in her heart—from having to deal with Cole and her grief. She couldn't even hear the wind blowing outside. But she could hear something else...

The garage had several stalls, and Xavier had a car in each. It sounded as if the engines of several of them were running now. Why?

Distracted, she stumbled against the rear bumper of one of the vehicles and struck her knee. Pain radiated up her leg, and a cry slipped through her lips. It was so dark without the lights.

She could barely remember which direction led to the house. The garage was attached to the French provincial mansion. That was why she'd rushed into it—because it had been close. She probably should have gone outside instead, like onto the expansive back patio or the wide front porch or the balcony on the second story.

But as desperate as she'd been for air, she hadn't wanted to see anyone else. Or more important, she hadn't wanted anyone else to see her.

To see how upset she was…

She'd had enough sympathy she didn't deserve. Being married to her had cost Emery his life. The bomb must have been meant for her—since it had been in her vehicle.

But why would anyone want *her* dead?

What had she done? Not that everyone liked her. Her family hadn't. And most of Cole's family didn't like her either. Not only did they suspect that Maisy might be another Bentler heir but they also did not like her close relationship with Xavier. All of Cole's cousins were as mean to her as her own had been. And she'd left her child alone in that house.

She needed to get back to Maisy and to Xavier.

As Shawna hurried past another car, she realized it was running, too, as was the one next to that, and the next one.

Fumes began to fill the garage. Exhaust. Carbon monoxide.

Why were the vehicles running?

Her eyes began to tear, and she coughed and sputtered for breath. Uncertain where the door to the house was, she turned back toward the outside door. She continued to cough as she rushed to it. Her hands trembling, she grabbed the knob.

But it didn't turn. She tugged and pulled at it. But

it didn't budge. Someone had locked the door—or blocked it—from the outside. She was trapped. Someone had trapped her inside a garage that was quickly filling with carbon monoxide. Someone definitely wanted her dead.

She could not die. She couldn't leave her child an orphan. But then Maisy wouldn't really be an orphan. She had a father still. Would Cole even want her?

Would he ever forgive Shawna for keeping her from him all these years? At the moment, his forgiveness was the last thing she needed to think about. Survival was paramount.

She was not the helpless damsel in distress Cole had once accused her of being. She was going to fight like hell to get out of here.

She was going to fight for Maisy...

I cannot live with what I've done. I am the one who planted the bomb that killed my husband. I wanted out of my marriage. Now I want out of my life.

Using the eraser of a pencil, the killer tapped out the message on the keys of Shawna Rolfe-Little's laptop keyboard. It would have to suffice. There was no way to print out the paper and have it signed—even if Shawna could have been coerced to sign it.

It was probably too late for that. Shawna might already be dead. She should already be dead.

If only Emery hadn't been the one to start her car...

It would have already been over, but then Little

would still be alive. The killer stared at the urn on the table in the library and felt no regret over his death. It wasn't as if Emery Little had been an innocent man. He'd been causing problems as well, problems that had pushed up the killer's timetable.

The plan had been to send Emery Little to prison, not the grave. Little was supposed to have been held responsible for Shawna's murder.

Plans could be adjusted, though. Now Shawna would be held responsible for Little's death and for her own. And Cole and his damn friends could return to wherever the hell they'd come from.

Cole turning up at the funeral had been a surprise. An unpleasant surprise.

But once Shawna was dead, he would have no reason to stay. She *had* to be dead.

Chapter 4

Where the hell is she?

Cole hadn't searched the entire house for her. The old mansion was too big for him to have investigated every nook and cranny. He had hit the main rooms first—the living room and dining room and parlors where the other mourners and unfortunately some of his scowling family members were hanging out. But he'd caught no sight of Shawna nor had any of his fellow bodyguards reported having seen her. They were all searching for her now, too.

Unsuccessfully.

How the hell had she just disappeared?

Cole retraced his steps to the library where he'd lost her. The pocket doors were open again, so more people—some of Cole's contemptuous cousins and his mom and his stepdad—had gone inside to pay their last respects to the urn of Emery Little's ashes.

He sucked in a breath at the sight of his mother. Tall and blonde and slender, Tiffani still looked like the pageant queen that she'd once been, the one who'd turned his father's head while working as an intern in his company. She didn't look old enough to be Cole's mother, but then she'd rarely acted like it.

She'd taken more to Shawna than she ever had him. They even used to work with the cheerleaders at the high school. He wondered if they still did that, but he didn't care enough to ask; that would have required approaching his mother. Since his father had died, they struggled to have any conversation at all, let alone a civil one.

His cousins—the female twins—Lori and Tori scowled at him. They tried to look like his mom by bleaching their hair and using colored contacts. They looked like caricatures of her instead. Then there were his male cousins, Bobby and Reggie, who were a little older than he was but still dressed and acted like frat boys, even at a funeral. They completely ignored him the way they'd done since they were all kids.

Jeffrey Inman, his stepfather, was the only one who paid him any attention. He waved at him and smiled. He seemed to be a nice man, and was also a former vet, retired now from the Army. But instead of heading toward him, Cole backed away from the open pocket doors.

Manny was in the library, too. Although the dark-haired bodyguard didn't know anyone beyond the descriptions of them that Cole had shared over the years, he was carrying on a couple of conversations. The bleached-blonde twins had latched onto him as if they had a chance with a man who was dating a supermodel. But Manny was friendly. He could talk to anyone or no one at all. As his roommate, Cole often heard the other man talking in his sleep.

At least he could sleep.

Cole struggled with that, with shutting off his mind enough to rest. Every time he closed his eyes, he saw things he spent his waking hours trying to forget. And it wasn't just the things that had happened during their missions.

He saw Shawna, too.

He saw way too much of Shawna when he closed his eyes. But when he opened his eyes, she was never there, never lying in bed next to him like he wanted her. Naked. Flushed with passion. Or smiling and affectionate. She was gone—just like she was now.

He realized that while he'd been searching for her, he hadn't seen her daughter either. They were probably together. Hadn't she sent Maisy off to check on his grandfather?

He backed out of the library and headed down the hallway toward the kitchen. The main meal had been set out as a buffet in the enormous dining room, but Cole had already been there and, as well as Shawna and Maisy, he hadn't seen Xavier either. Of course it would have been more difficult for the old man to sneak treats off the buffet. The excess bakery goods had been left sitting out in the kitchen, and his grandfather's sweet tooth was legendary.

But when Cole stepped into the kitchen, he found it empty, as well. The cook and servers must have been in the dining room, restocking the buffet. Some of the cookies were gone, but for one that Cole crunched under his foot against the tile floor. He glanced down and noticed a few more had fallen onto the tiles near the long island that ran between the rows of cabinets on each wall. As he leaned down to pick them up, he noticed little feet sticking out between two bar stools pulled up beneath the granite counter.

He dropped to his haunches and met the blue-eyed gaze of the little girl who sat with her back against the cabinets and her knobby knees pulled up nearly to her chin. Cookie crumbs clung to her lips and liberally peppered her black tights. Although it was obvious, he asked, "Whatcha doing?"

Tears welled in her eyes. She squeezed her lids shut, but some of those tears slipped through her thick black lashes. Cole gasped as he felt that sensation he used to feel when Shawna cried, like someone was squeezing his heart in a tight fist. Needing to comfort her—and maybe himself as well—he scooped her out from beneath the counter and into his arms. Maisy's eyes opened and she stared up at him through her tears.

"Are you okay?" he asked, then grimaced at his insensitivity. Of course she wasn't okay. She'd lost her father. He had to make sure she didn't lose her mother, too.

But everyone was searching for Shawna. Someone would find her soon—probably more easily than he would since he was the one from whom she'd run away.

"That was a stupid thing to ask you, huh?" he remarked.

She blinked again, but no more tears fell. "Why?" she asked.

"Because I know what's wrong," he said. And it wasn't just the fact that she had probably eaten too many cookies. "My dad died, too."

She lifted her hand to his cheek like she had in the library. But now she was offering him comfort. "I'm sorry," she said. "That's what everyone keeps saying to me...like it's their fault." Her blue eyes widened with fear. "Is it?"

It was somebody's fault, unless Emery Little had set that bomb himself. And Cole doubted that. The man had had everything to live for. He'd had a great job with students who adored him. And he had a wonderful little girl. And he'd had Shawna.

Where the hell was Shawna?

A chill chased down his spine as he thought of her and of what Maisy had just said. Had her father's killer apologized to her? Was he or she somebody in this very house?

"I don't know whose fault it is," he answered honestly. "But I will find out." Damn. He'd just made another promise, but for some reason he felt compelled to take care of her, just like he'd felt compelled to take care of Shawna when they'd first met so many years ago.

"Do you know who killed your daddy?" she asked.

He shook his head. "Nobody killed him." Except himself. "It was an accident."

His father had been so driven, so determined to get as much out of life as possible that he'd lived it on the edge. It shouldn't have been so surprising that he had eventually fallen off. Literally. He'd lost control of his sports car on a sharp turn and had fallen off a cliff. There hadn't been much more of him left than there had been of Emery Little.

"My dad died several years ago," he told her. "It gets easier."

"Easier?" she parroted, her little brow puckered with confusion.

It probably hadn't been the right word to use.

"Better." He shrugged. "I don't know. It just gradually hurts less."

She released a little breath. "That's good. Will Mommy hurt less, too?"

That tight fist squeezed his heart again. He hated to think of Shawna in pain, especially and selfishly, over another man. "Yeah, eventually."

The little girl's wide eyes narrowed as she studied his face. Did she see his jealousy? She was much too astute. How could she be barely five years old?

"She'll be okay," he assured the little girl.

"But aren't you supposed to be bodyguarding her?" Maisy asked.

"Well…" That was damn hard to do when you couldn't find the body you were supposed to be guarding.

"You promised," she reminded him.

"Yes, I did," he said. But he wasn't certain if that

was a promise that Shawna would make it possible for him to keep. "But I don't know where she's gone."

"I know," she said.

But before she could tell him, Manny burst into the kitchen, a laptop tightly clenched in his hands. "There you are!" he exclaimed. "You've got to see this." Then he noticed the little girl in Cole's arms and his face flushed. "But she shouldn't—if she can read."

"What? What is it?" Maisy asked.

But Cole put her down on the floor and held the laptop above her head, just in case she could read already. He shook his head at the supposed suicide note where Shawna admitted her guilt. "No..."

It wasn't possible.

If Shawna was capable of killing anyone, it would have been him when he'd broken their engagement six years ago. She had been furious with him then. More furious than he had ever seen her...even more than when she'd stormed out on him a short time ago.

"What is it?" Maisy asked again as she tugged on his arm.

"Nothing," Cole said. Then he remembered. "You said you know where your mother went—tell me!"

At the urgency in his voice, the color drained from the little girl's already pale face, and her bottom lip quivered as if she was about to cry. That was the last thing Cole had wanted to cause. He wanted to make sure she didn't have any reason to cry, ever again.

He dropped to his knees beside her. "It's okay," he said. "You can tell me where your mother is. Remember—I'm supposed to be bodyguarding her."

He could only hope that when he found Shawna,

it wasn't too late to save her. Why would the killer have written a suicide note to frame her, unless that killer was damn certain that she was already dead?

Panic pressed on Shawna's lungs, which already burned from the carbon monoxide filling the garage. Thankfully the building was big, with a tall ceiling, or she might have died already.

Eyes streaming from the toxic fumes, she blinked furiously as she searched through the darkness and smoke for the control panel that opened the overhead doors from the inside. She found it near the service door to the house—the one that, just like the back door, would not open. It had been locked somehow from the outside.

Her fingers shaking, she pressed the buttons for all the overhead doors but none of them budged. And of course the lights were off. Someone must have cut the power to the garage.

There was no way out without knocking down a door. And she just wasn't strong enough. Cole's voice echoed inside her head, taunting her like her cousins used to taunt her. *Damsel in distress. Damsel in distress.*

No. It wasn't that she wasn't strong enough to break down a door. She wasn't big enough. She was stronger than Cole knew, stronger for which he'd given her credit. And while she couldn't bust her way out of the garage physically, she could do it mentally.

Couldn't she?

Her vision began to blur and not just from the smoke and the darkness. Her lungs burning, she was beginning to lose consciousness. She couldn't do that or she would lose it all.

Her life. Maisy...

Thinking of her sweet little girl renewed her strength. She stumbled through the smoke toward one of those cars and pulled at the driver's door. It was locked with the damn keys in the ignition.

She stumbled into another bay, toward another door, but it was locked, as well. How had someone managed to start all the vehicles without Astin knowing?

Where was the chauffeur?

She stumbled toward another vehicle but tripped as her feet hit something. And she fell. A body broke her landing, saving her from the concrete on which Astin lay. His hat had been knocked off, and blood spattered the ground and the side of the nearest vehicle.

"Oh, no!" she gasped. And more tears burned her eyes, but these weren't from the fumes. Astin was such a sweet man. And like anyone who worked for Xavier, he had become part of the family— dysfunctional though it was. She felt his wrist, hoping to find a pulse. And her breath shuddered out when she found one, albeit weak. She leaned closer, making sure that he was still breathing.

He was. But barely. He needed air. And so did she. She wasn't certain she would have been able to perform CPR, had he stopped breathing.

She had to get them out.

She pushed herself to her feet again and as she did, her hands scraped the concrete and something metal. A crowbar lay next to the chauffeur's body.

She wrapped her fingers around it but it was harder to lift than she'd thought it would be.

And she could barely think…

Her mind was so foggy, like the air in the garage. She couldn't see. She could barely stand, her legs threatened to fold beneath her. But she couldn't give up.

She had to find a way out. A way back to her daughter.

Gathering all her strength, she lifted the crowbar and swung it at the car door. It bounced off the car window and fell from her grasp, clamoring to the concrete beside the vehicle.

What the hell was the glass made of? Why wouldn't it break? Was she just that weak?

Coughing and sputtering, she dropped to her knees to pick the bar back up. But she couldn't summon the strength to stand again. Her legs—all of her muscles—felt like jelly.

She was so weak and foggy-headed that she thought of lying down beside Astin. Wouldn't Cole come to her rescue like he always had?

Then again, she'd told him she didn't want his protection. She didn't need his help. She'd lied to him and to herself. But she'd had no idea—until now—just how much danger she was in…

The bomb hadn't been a mistake, except that it had claimed Emery's life instead of hers. Someone clearly wanted her dead. And she was afraid that someone might be about to get his wish.

"We need a crowbar," Manny said as he struggled with the service door on the side of the garage.

Fumes seeped out from beneath it into the mudroom that separated the house from the garage in which vehicles rumbled. Someone had locked the door from the inside, and he could guess who.

But it was clear that Cole, who'd shaken his head as he'd read the suicide note, refused to accept it. Maybe he was right to be suspicious of it, though.

Because it wasn't a lock on the inside keeping the door closed but a lock on the outside, a lock that had been filled with some kind of industrial strength glue. It stuck to Manny's palms as he wrestled with the knob. He cursed and kicked at the door.

Fortunately, it wasn't the only one in the mudroom. Another door opened onto the sidewalk to the driveway. Cole rushed through it and around to the front of the garage. Smoke furled beneath the overhead doors, too, seeping out.

Cole tugged at the handle of one, but he couldn't raise it. And as he struggled with it, Manny heard one of those rumbling engines roar as someone pressed on an accelerator. Wood splintered and tires squealed as the vehicle barreled through the door.

And through Cole?

He didn't see his friend, who moments before had been standing in front of that door. He only saw the long, black limousine that had rammed through it. And he saw behind the wheel of that vehicle, the woman with long black hair.

She wasn't dead.

But she might have just killed Cole.

Chapter 5

Cole's shoulder ached from where he'd hit the concrete—hard—when he'd dodged out of the way of the oncoming vehicle. After breaking through the door, the long, black vintage limousine didn't stop but continued to accelerate down the driveway before crashing into a parked car. Glass shattered and metal crunched and then a car horn blared.

He rolled to his feet and rushed toward the crash site. The vehicle that the limousine had hit was a crunched-up mass of broken metal and plastic. Thankfully no one was inside it.

Unfortunately someone was inside the limousine. And while it had fared better than the smaller car, the front of it was smashed, steam or smoke unfurling from beneath its hood. If it was about to catch fire, he needed to get the driver out.

His hands shaking as adrenaline and fear coursed through him, he reached for the door handle. While it wasn't locked, the door refused to open. The fender had crumpled up against the hinges, making them inoperable. He stared through the driver's window, which had either been broken or smashed out. All he could see of Shawna was her hair, which covered her face as she lay over the steering wheel.

The limousine was old, so old that it had no air-bags. There had been nothing to cushion the force of the crash—nothing to protect her.

But him...

He was supposed to have protected her. He was her bodyguard. He hadn't done a very damn good job of it yet, though.

He reached through the window and slid his fingers through her hair until he found her throat. At first he felt no pulse, but he moved his hand and felt a faint throbbing beneath her skin.

"Thank God," he murmured. Maisy couldn't lose her mother. Not so soon after losing her father. But Shawna wasn't safe yet. He had no idea the extent of her injuries. So he didn't dare move her.

He glanced again to the front of the car and determined it was definitely steam curling out of the smashed radiator and not smoke rising from the hood.

He kept his hand on her throat, to make sure her pulse didn't stop entirely, and he used his other hand to pull out his cell phone and call 911. "Send an ambulance to this address..." He heard the dispatcher's gasp when he gave it. His grandfather was well-known. Probably too well-known. "A thirty-year-old female is unconscious but has a weak pulse. She's been in an accident."

"This was no accident," Manny said as he joined him. "And we need two ambulances. There's a man in the garage with a head wound and probably lungs full of carbon monoxide. Dane's administering CPR right now, but I don't know if he'll make it."

Cole's heart flipped. Was it his grandfather? He hadn't seen the old man when he'd been looking for Shawna. Had they been together in that garage full of running vehicles?

Despite the dispatcher sputtering in his ear to remain on the line until help arrived, Cole disconnected the call and turned to his friend.

"Who is it?" he asked as he peered back at the garage. Through the smashed door, he could only see the other Payne Protection bodyguards crouched around whoever was lying on the concrete.

"From the uniform," Manny said, "it looks like the chauffeur."

"Astin…" Cole felt no relief that it wasn't his grandfather. The chauffeur had been in Xavier's employ for so long that he was family, too—better family than most of Cole's blood relatives had been to him.

Manny gestured inside the limousine.

Cole peered through the window and caught the glint of metal. On the passenger seat next to her lay a crowbar, smeared with blood.

"Do you think she hit him?" Manny asked.

Cole shook his head. "No. No way."

Manny snorted. "What the hell's wrong with you?"

"What?" He wasn't the one unconscious in a crashed car. But was it the crash that had caused Shawna to pass out or was it the carbon monoxide?

"She needs oxygen," he said. Like Astin did. A pang struck his heart. The chauffeur couldn't die. And neither could Shawna. "We need to move her."

"Did you lose her pulse?" Manny asked.

Cole shook his head. Not yet. But he could feel her slipping away. "We need to be ready to start CPR, though."

"We shouldn't move her until the paramedics get here," Manny disagreed. "They'll have a neck brace."

Cole nodded. "You're right." He couldn't risk paralyzing her. He had to be patient. In the distance he could hear sirens wailing. "You're right."

"Did you hit your head?" Manny asked.

"What?" Cole asked.

"When she ran you over, did you hit your head on the ground?" Manny asked. It didn't sound like Manny was actually concerned about Cole's health, more like he was concerned about his sanity. Manny studied his face, his dark eyes narrowed and intense.

"I did not hit my head," Cole informed his friend slowly and succinctly. "I am fine."

Manny shook his head. "No. You're not. You're in trouble here."

"What? Why?" Distracted with concern for Shawna and Astin, Cole couldn't figure out if his friend was goofing around like they usually did, even during the most stressful times, or if he was seriously worried.

"You're in trouble because you can't be objective," Manny explained. "You're not thinking with your head at all. You're thinking with your heart."

Cole sucked in a breath as concern struck his heart. Manny was right. He was dangerously close to falling for Shawna all over again—and for her mini-me daughter, as well.

"She left a note," Manny continued. "She confessed—"

"She did not write that note," Cole interrupted. "She didn't kill her husband. And she sure as hell did not just try to kill herself or Astin."

The chauffeur had driven them to homecoming dances and prom. He had always been an important part of their lives. Shawna would never hurt him.

Now as for whether she would hurt Cole…

Nearly running him down might not have been an accident. She was still furious with him for the things he'd said when he broke up with her. And he could hardly blame her.

"Remember how you realized six years ago that she wasn't the woman you thought she was?" Manny persisted. "The minute you broke up with her, she married someone else, someone you didn't even know she was seeing. You don't know her at all. You never did."

Pain jabbed Cole's heart as his friend's words sank in. Manny was right. Shawna had never been the woman Cole had thought she was. Because he'd thought she'd been a woman in love with him—so in love with him that he hadn't wanted to put her through his death if he hadn't survived that mission.

But he'd survived. And she had thrived without him. No. He hadn't known her at all.

Could she be a killer, though?

Had she killed him?

Shawna remembered those last moments before she'd lost consciousness. She remembered using all that had been left of her strength to push down on the accelerator and send the limo crashing through the garage door.

And she remembered Cole, his body flying through the air. Had she hit him?

Over and over behind her closed lids, she kept replaying that image of Cole. Of the shock on his face as she crashed through that door. And into him?

Seeing him was the last thing she remembered, seeing him flying. Her head pounded as she tried to remember what had happened to him. Had she seen him again?

She remembered flashing lights and voices, remembered being in a hospital. She'd insisted on coming home. Hadn't she? The most recent parts of her memory—after crashing through that door—were the haziest to her.

She didn't even know where she was. And worse yet, she didn't know what had happened to Cole or to her daughter. She jerked awake with a cry. "Maisy!"

"Shhh," rumbled a deep voice, choked with emotion. "She's all right. And you're all right now. We've brought you home."

When she blinked her eyes open, she wasn't home in the little bungalow she'd shared with Emery and her daughter. The room she was in had heavy draperies pulled at the windows, darkening it but for the pool of light cast by the Tiffany lamp on the bedside table. She was in her room in Xavier Bentler's mansion, and Xavier was the one sitting next to her bed, holding her hand in his. His skin was wrinkled and spotted with age, but his grip was surprisingly strong despite his more than eight decades of living.

She was supposed to be his nurse. Instead he appeared to be acting as hers. "Cole..." His name was just a croak from her scratchy throat.

How long had she been asleep?

"He's just outside the door," Xavier said. "I'll get him for you."

She held tightly to his hand before he could pull away from her. "No, no, I don't need him," she murmured in a whisper. She just wanted to make sure he was all right. "Did I—did I hit him?"

Xavier chuckled. "Did you want to?"

She shook her head.

"Then you have nothing to worry about," he assured her as he patted her hand. "He jumped out of the way." He released a little shuddery sigh. "God knows if he didn't have quick reflexes, he wouldn't have made it back to us from all those missions."

She shook her head again. He hadn't made it back to her, and he never would. He wouldn't have been home at all if not for Xavier hiring the Payne Protection Agency and forcing him to return. Before she could say anything more, though, the bedroom door creaked open.

"Is she awake?" a deep voice asked.

It wasn't Cole; he stood behind the man who spoke. This guy had black hair and startling blue eyes. He'd been with Cole and his other friends at the church.

"I'm awake," she said.

"I'm Cooper Payne," he introduced himself.

"He runs the security company that I hired to protect you," Xavier chimed in. "Can't say I'm all that impressed, Payne. We nearly lost her and Astin."

"Astin," she gasped as she remembered finding the chauffeur lying on the ground. "Is he all right?" She felt so guilty. She'd been so worried about Cole that she'd nearly forgotten about Astin.

Xavier's breath shuddered out in a sigh of relief. "Yes, thank God he's got a hard head. They're keeping him in the hospital to make sure he has no swelling and to treat his lungs."

Not just his lungs. Depending on the amount of carbon monoxide he'd inhaled, he could have organ failure. "Do they have him in a hyperbaric chamber?"

"A what?" Xavier asked.

"Pressured oxygen chamber," she said. That would have been the appropriate treatment given his exposure to the carbon monoxide. He must have been inside the garage when whoever started all those cars was in there. Her treatment, which she only vaguely remembered, would have been pure oxygen through a mask. She could faintly recall pulling at it as she'd tried to talk.

Xavier nodded. "Yeah, yeah, that's what it is." As

if trying to convince himself, he added, "He should be fine."

Should be...

But there was no guarantee. The carbon monoxide could have damaged his heart or his brain. As an ER nurse, she'd seen other cases, and shuddered at the thought of having been one herself. "But if he hasn't regained consciousness yet..." He might never.

Cooper Payne spoke up, "He did come around just a short time ago."

"Thank God," Xavier said, and it was clear he hadn't been as certain as he'd tried to sound that his old friend and employee would be okay.

"One of my men is at the hospital and spoke with him when he regained consciousness," Cooper continued. "He says he didn't see who struck him." But those blue eyes narrowed with suspicion as he studied her face.

He wasn't the only one looking at her that way. There was another dark-haired man with him, standing beside Cole. His dark eyes scrutinized her face with clear suspicion and even a trace of hostility.

She thought she'd met him before—when she'd met some of the men with whom Cole had served. Was his name Manny? Her head pounded as she tried to remember. But more important than his name, why was he looking at her that way?

"I—I didn't see who hit him either," she said. "I found him lying on the ground when I was trying to get out of the garage."

"You were trying to get out." Cole finally spoke but it was more to his friends than to her.

"Of course I was," she said, and she coughed as her dry throat tickled.

"She needs to rest," Xavier said. "You're not going to interrogate her now."

"We're not the only ones with questions," Payne replied. "The police want to talk to her, too, about what happened. And we can't protect her if we don't know what's really going on."

She flinched as the pounding in her head intensified. She felt like she'd been hit in the head like Astin had. She was lucky she hadn't been though, or she might not have survived.

"She's in pain," Cole spoke again. "Grandfather's right. We can't interrogate her now."

One of the men—Manny—snorted. "She nearly ran you over, and you don't want to know what's going on."

"I don't know," she murmured. But she wanted to know why someone wanted to kill her. She focused on Cole's handsome face. "I didn't try to run you over," she told him. "I was just trying to get out of that garage."

"The doctor said you were lucky you escaped when you did," Xavier said. "He also said that you certainly saved Astin's life by breaking down that door."

If Astin survived…

If the chauffeur didn't survive, then someone else would have died because of her. And if she'd struck Cole…

She stared at him. "You're sure you're all right? I saw you flying."

"I jumped," Cole said. "You didn't hit me."

"Did you want to?" Manny asked her but not with the amusement that Xavier had. He asked with real suspicion.

She gasped.

And Cole shoved his friend's shoulder. "Hey—"

"You, of all people, shouldn't trust her," Manny said.

And her heart flipped over. Had they figured out that Maisy was Cole's child? Did they know she'd kept that secret for all these years? That she'd kept him from his daughter? If so, they would have every reason to distrust and resent her.

She focused again on Cole's handsome face, but she saw no sign of anger or betrayal. And certainly if he knew the truth, he would hate her. So she turned toward his friend. "What are you talking about?"

Of course he was Cole's friend. Maybe, like Cole, he was disgusted that she'd married another man so soon after their breakup. But it hadn't been her choice to end their engagement; that had been Cole's.

"I found the note on your laptop," Manny said.

She glanced to the bedside table where she'd probably had it last. But the computer was gone. "What— Where is it?"

"With our computer expert now," Manny replied. "But I found it in the library, where you left it next to the urn of your dead husband's ashes."

She flinched as she thought of Emery. This day was supposed to be about him, about memorializing him. Instead it had become about her and Cole and poor Astin. She shook her head and struggled to sit up and swing her legs over the bed. "I didn't leave it there."

"I told you," Cole said. "It's a setup."

"What?" What was a setup? What were they talking about?

But the two men ignored her question as they focused on each other. Cole continued, "If she intended to kill herself, she wouldn't have fought so hard to escape from the garage."

"Kill myself?" she gasped.

Xavier turned back to her and patted her arm. "It's fine, honey, nobody believes you killed Emery."

"Emery?" Was she really awake? Or was she caught in some nightmare from which she couldn't wake up? "I—I don't understand."

She hadn't killed Emery. But he was dead because of her. Because someone wanted her dead.

Why?

"You didn't write the confession-slash-suicide note I found on your laptop?" Manny asked.

Panic gripped her like it had in the garage when she couldn't breathe. She couldn't breathe now either. Confession? Suicide?

"I would never—ever—do that. To myself or to my daughter." Thinking of Maisy gave her the strength to kick off the blankets and get out of bed. And just as she did, the door opened, and the little girl rushed into the room.

"Mommy!" Tears stained her cheeks. "You're okay!"

Shawna pulled the little girl into her arms and held

her closely to her chest—to her heart. "Yes, sweetheart, I'm okay."

But she worried that she wouldn't be much longer. This killer that was after her, that had already killed, was ruthless and determined. And while she was no damsel in distress, Shawna wasn't certain how much longer she would be able to fight for her life.

Nikki Payne shook her head. "No. I don't think she could have written that letter."

She didn't miss the look of relief on Cole's face. His shoulders lifted slightly, too, as if his burden had been partially eased. She knew it wasn't gone, though. His jaw was still clenched, the tension evident.

"I don't think it was written until after she was locked in the garage," Nikki said. "And I confirmed what Manny suspected, that the service door locks were tampered with. Looks like superglue."

"And she couldn't have done that herself either," Cole added.

Nikki shook her head again. Manny had had an answer for that. He suspected she'd tampered with those locks before letting herself into the garage through an open overhead door.

But the power had been cut to the garage so she would have had to manually pull down that door. And they were too big, too high for Shawna to have pulled down. Nikki, who was just as petite, had tested Manny's theory when she inspected the garage after they all left for the hospital.

Fortunately the garage was big, or it would have filled up with carbon monoxide so fast that Shawna wouldn't have had the chance to escape. Nikki respected the recent widow's resourcefulness.

"We were all searching the house for her," Nikki reminded Cole. "We would have seen her go back to put the laptop in the library."

He nodded. "Yes, because like I told you, it wasn't there when she and I were in there together. Or I would have seen it sitting next to the urn."

"Yeah, someone tried to set her up for her husband's murder and for her own death."

"And Astin's, if he doesn't make it."

It was still touch and go with the chauffeur. Lars had spoken to him at the hospital, but he'd said the doctor had warned he was still in critical condition.

"If only he'd seen something."

"Someone must have," Cole insisted. "The killer was in this house—in her room—in the library." He glanced to the closed door of her bedroom.

Shawna and her daughter were alone in there.

Nikki saw the fear on his face, but she wondered if he was only afraid for them or if he was afraid for himself, as well. One man had died because of her and another had nearly died. Cole could lose his life, too.

Or was it his heart he was afraid of losing?

Chapter 6

Cole glanced around the library at the faces of his family. Some, like his stepfather and mother, appeared concerned. Some seemed resentful, like his cousins. His uncles, Ronald and Lawrence, just looked uninterested in anyone or anything beyond themselves.

No one aroused his suspicion. But it had to be one of them. He'd come to that conclusion when he'd talked to Nikki just moments ago. A member of his family had tried to kill Shawna, had nearly killed Astin and had already killed Emery Little.

His urn sat among them, but nobody looked at it. Out of guilt? No. Cole doubted the killer felt any remorse for what he'd done. Or he wouldn't have been so determined to make Maisy an orphan.

What would happen to her if she lost both of her

parents? Emery had had students and friends come to mourn him, but Cole couldn't remember seeing any family—parents or siblings—that might care for the little girl. And Shawna really had no one. After how her aunt and cousins had treated her, he doubted she would name any of them as guardian for her daughter.

A pang struck his heart at the thought of the little girl being all alone in the world. Earlier she'd sought him out for comfort when he'd returned from the hospital with her mother, who'd insisted on coming home to her daughter. Shawna hadn't wanted to be apart from Maisy.

And now neither did he. Without a word to any of his family, he slipped out of the library and headed up the stairs to the second floor and the wing where Shawna was staying. It wasn't safe for her to be here.

Nikki was still outside the door, and although she was the smallest of all the Payne Protection bodyguards, she'd proven she could be lethal when necessary. She was good.

But Cole wasn't reassured. He had to see for himself that Maisy and her mother were all right. And he had to convince Shawna to leave this house, to leave his family.

Why was she still involved with them?

And when he pushed open the door, he remembered why. His grandfather. He sat beside Shawna's bed yet, reading a story to Maisy. It was obvious he didn't just have a connection with Shawna but with her daughter, too.

Why?

He studied the little girl closely. Could she be his?

He shook his head. No. Shawna had told him that Maisy was too young. Hadn't she said that?

He couldn't remember her exact words now. But he knew that was what she'd meant when the thought had first crossed his mind that Maisy could be his. That the last time they'd made love had been too long before she'd given birth. The last time they'd made love…

His body heated and tensed as he thought of the passion, of the hunger.

He'd known then that it would have to be the last time, so he'd made it count. He'd savored and committed to memory every kiss, every caress, every stroke.

"Hey, Cole!" Maisy said when she noticed him. "Are you here to guard Mommy some more?"

He nodded, even though he wasn't sure Shawna had decided to allow that yet. Earlier that day, before she'd run off to the garage and her almost demise, she had been adamant about him not being her bodyguard.

She didn't argue now. Or maybe she just didn't intend to do that in front of her daughter and his grandfather. "It's late," she said, speaking to the little girl, "Well past your bedtime. You need to get your pajamas on and brush your teeth and then I'll tuck you in. Okay?"

Maisy hesitated. "I don't want to leave you, Mommy."

"I need to talk to Cole for a few minutes and I'll be right here," Shawna assured her.

"I'll go help you find your pajamas," his grandfather offered.

He rose spryly from his chair with the little girl in his arms. How did he have so much strength and energy still at his age? The man never ceased to amaze or frustrate Cole. As they passed him, Xavier squeezed his shoulder. And Cole stared into his face at the new lines there. The old man was worried. He had to know what Cole had just realized. Someone in their family was a cold-blooded killer.

But he waited until Xavier closed the door to share his revelation with Shawna. "You shouldn't be here," he told her.

"The doctor released me," she said.

"Only because you and my grandfather insisted," he said. At the time, he'd thought it would be easier to keep her safe here than at the hospital. He'd been wrong. "But that's not what I'm talking about. You shouldn't be in this house. It's too dangerous."

She tensed, and her dark eyes widened with fear. "What are you talking about?"

"The attempt on your life," he replied. "The attempted frame-up to make it look like you killed your husband and then intended to commit suicide."

She shuddered. "That's ridiculous."

It was more than that. "It's too dangerous for you to be here," he insisted.

"I—I can't go home," she said. "The explosion… It damaged the house."

He approached the bed and took the seat his grandfather had vacated next to her. But he didn't reach for her hand like Xavier had. He didn't dare touch her—

not with how fiercely his heart was already pounding. He was afraid for her and for Maisy. But he was also afraid for himself.

For how she made him feel.

She looked so vulnerable lying in bed. Her porcelain skin was even paler than usual but for the dark circles beneath her dark eyes.

"Of course you can't go back there," he agreed. "But you can't stay here either. It's not safe."

Tears welled in her eyes then, but she furiously blinked, obviously trying to fight them. She was a fighter. She'd proven that today when she'd escaped the garage full of carbon monoxide.

Cole needed to do a better job of protecting her from all kind of harm. "I'm sorry," he said. "I didn't mean to upset you."

Her eyes widened then and she incredulously asked, "Really?"

"I've been hired to protect you," he said. "Not hurt you."

Him being here hurt her—a lot. Just seeing his face, being this close to him, made Shawna ache for all the years they'd lost. She had missed him so much. She'd missed seeing him, touching him.

Kissing him.

Making love with him...

Her body ached for his. And her heart ached with the pain he'd caused her. She would never be able to trust him again. She couldn't let him get close enough to hurt her again—because she was certain that he would, just like he had six years ago. She leaned away from him, pressing her back against the headboard.

"I already said I don't want you as my bodyguard," she reminded him. And herself.

For those long moments she'd been trapped in the garage, she'd reconsidered that choice. She'd regretted running away from him.

"You can't deny that you need protection," he told her, his voice gruff with frustration.

"I can't," she agreed. "I just don't want you."

Liar.

Her heart called her on it. She wanted him. Too much. That was the problem.

"I want to talk to your boss," she said. When Cooper Payne had been in her room earlier, she should have told him then to assign someone else as her bodyguard. But his and Manny's questions and suspicions had taken her by surprise. The only one who'd believed she was innocent was Cole.

How would the others protect her if they didn't believe she was really in danger? And getting locked in the garage had proved to her that she was, that the car explosion had only been a mistake in that it had claimed Emery's life instead of hers.

"Cooper is my friend," Cole told her. "He's not going to honor your wishes over mine."

She arched a brow with skepticism. "Really? Didn't he honor Xavier's wishes over yours? Your friend took this assignment despite knowing how you'd feel about it, how you feel about me…"

Cole sighed. "Maybe he did. But he was right to take this assignment. And no matter what happened between us six years ago, I don't want you hurt." He reached out then and trailed his fingertips over her cheek. "Or worse."

She blinked again, fighting those damn tears. Maybe it was an aftereffect of all that carbon monoxide that had her eyes burning. Or maybe it was fatigue.

Or emotion.

"That's why you need to leave here," he said.

But she had nowhere else to go. Her relationships with her aunt and cousins had never improved enough for her to infringe on their hospitality ever again.

"Why don't you want me here?" she asked. Was it because he'd broken up with her? Didn't he even want her around his family? She wasn't exactly thrilled to be here either. But she'd never been able to say no his grandfather. And Xavier needed her, or so he'd claimed.

"It's not safe," Cole said. "You must realize that after the attempt on your life. It has to be one of *them.*"

Maybe the carbon monoxide had damaged her brain because she wasn't following him. "One of them? One of who?"

His voice was gruff with emotion when he replied, "My family."

She shook her head. "Why would you think that?"

Despite how his family had treated him, it was clearly tough for him to consider that one of them could be a killer. "Because the attempt happened here."

"During a memorial service that most of the town

attended," she reminded him. "Your family members were not the only people with access to this house today."

He expelled a slight, ragged sigh. "That's true."

She couldn't help herself, seeing the pain on his face that his suspicions had brought him. She reached out and touched his cheek. Stubble had begun to form along his jaw, and it tickled her fingertips, making her skin tingle. Her breath caught and she forgot what she'd intended to say.

He covered her hand with his, but instead of pulling it away, he held it against his face, as if savoring her touch. His blue eyes darkened as he stared at her. Then he leaned closer.

And warmth spread through Shawna's heart. No matter how much he'd hurt her, she still reacted to him, to his closeness. To his attractiveness. He was so damn good-looking that it wasn't fair—not to her heart.

She closed her eyes just as his lips brushed over hers. The kiss was gentle, just a soft caress and mingling of breaths. Then he pulled her hand from his face and his mouth was gone. She would have thought she'd just imagined that kiss but for the tingling of her lips now. When she opened her eyes, she found him standing near the door—his hand on the handle of the gun protruding from his holster.

The door burst open and Maisy ran inside, jumping onto the bed with her. Shawna saw the flash of metal of the gun Cole had drawn as he hastily re-holstered it. Her heart pounded fast now with fear. Cole could have shot his own child.

She needed to tell him the truth while she had the chance. If something happened to her, she couldn't leave Maisy alone. Her child wouldn't be an orphan the way she had been.

Maisy still had her father.

Before Shawna could say anything to him, he was gone, slipping through the door Maisy had left open. Before it closed, she caught a glimpse of him talking to a curly-haired woman in the hallway.

The woman had been with him and the other men at the church and at the house today for the memorial brunch. Who was she? Just another bodyguard? Or something more to Cole?

Shawna felt a flash of jealousy, but she had no right to it. She'd married another man, even though they'd had an unusual arrangement. Cole was the only man she'd ever been with and the only one she wanted to be with—even now.

"Where did Cole go?" Maisy asked as she snuggled into Shawna's arms.

She held her daughter close and murmured, "I don't know."

"I thought he was supposed to be bodyguarding you but Miss Nikki is outside the door."

Miss Nikki? The petite brunette was a bodyguard?

Shawna suppressed a snort of derision. She doubted that. But she wouldn't express those doubts to her daughter. She wanted Maisy to think she was safe, even though she didn't believe it herself.

She was in danger for her life.

And thanks to that brief kiss, her heart, as well.

Manny hadn't much family of his own, at least not family that wasn't locked up behind bars. So he appreciated Cole's more than Cole apparently did. He had yet to see his friend talk to any of them besides his grandfather.

That old codger was a badass, and if Manny believed the man's family, a manipulative bastard, as well. He had manipulated Cole to get him back home. Why?

Just to protect Shawna? Or to reunite them?

Manny still had his doubts about the young widow. Sure, Nikki had pretty much proven that she couldn't have tried to kill herself or the chauffeur. But what about her husband?

Manny stared at the urn containing what was left of the poor guy. Everyone thought that he'd just been an innocent bystander caught in the crossfire—collateral damage. What if he'd actually been the intended victim?

Bombs weren't hard to figure out how to make. All the improvised explosive devices he'd encountered during his deployments had proved that. Shawna seemed like a shrewd woman, shrewd enough to escape that garage. She could have figured out how to fabricate that bomb.

When Cole joined him, he shared that thought with him. And, predictably, his friend bristled. "What the hell is your problem with her?" he asked. "Why do you want to think the worst of her?"

"To protect you," Manny answered honestly.

Cole snorted. "I've been in a lot more dangerous situations than this. So have you."

Just recently Manny had been in the most danger of his life and it hadn't just been physical. He'd fallen for a woman way out of his league. And if Teddie

Plummer hadn't fallen for him just as hard, he would have been destroyed.

Like he worried Shawna would destroy Cole. Again.

"All those dangerous missions we went on never affected you like she did," Manny said. "Nobody ever hurt you like she did." Cole hadn't talked about Shawna often, but when he had, it was always with pain.

Cole shook his head. "I'm the one who broke the engagement."

"But she's the one who broke your heart."

Cole didn't deny that. He just stared at that urn as if Emery Little held any answers. The man was dead. Shawna had hurt him, too. Either intentionally or inadvertently.

Manny wanted to protect his friend. That was why he debated sharing what else he'd learned from Cole's family. Would it make him see that he couldn't trust her? Or would it draw him back into her web?

"I've been talking to your family," he began.

And Cole snorted again. "Yeah, I've noticed. I was surprised to find you alone in here."

"Most of them are in the den," Manny said, "unless they've gone upstairs to bed." He couldn't imagine so much family under one roof. But then this was an enormous roof.

He thought of the small apartment he shared with Cole, when the guy was used to places like this. As he'd suspected, his friend must have found the cramped, attic apartment because he'd known the rent would be affordable for Manny. Cole could afford anything.

Except getting his heart broken again.

Manny was Cole's friend and even if he wasn't, he would have struggled to keep anything secret. "A lot of your family think that little girl is yours," he admitted.

The cousins had reluctantly shared their suspicions while Cole's mother had been proud to claim that the little girl was probably her granddaughter.

Cole snorted again. "I'm surprised they'd admit to the possibility of another Bentler heir."

"They don't seem happy about it," Manny said, "except for your mother and stepfather. They'd be thrilled to be grandparents."

"They're not," Cole said. "She's not."

Manny pointed at the picture beside the urn. "He has dark eyes. So does Shawna. But the little girl…"

Cole audibly sucked in a breath.

Knowing his friend had braced himself, Manny braced himself. He knew that his friends weren't above throwing a punch when provoked. "She has *your* eyes."

But Cole didn't hit him. He didn't even curse. He just spun on his heel and left the library and Manny, the urn and the picture of Emery Little behind him. Manny had no doubt that Cole was furious. But that anger wasn't directed at him.

No, Cole held all that fury for someone else.

The woman who'd broken his heart and deprived him of five years of his daughter's life? Manny hoped so, but then he felt a stab of guilt.

He hadn't wanted to cause trouble. He only wanted to protect his friend from a woman who had already hurt him once. Manny wanted to make sure she didn't get the opportunity to hurt Cole again.

Then again, Manny wasn't the only one trying to

take that opportunity away from Shawna Rolfe-Little. But no matter how she'd treated Cole, she didn't deserve to die.

Manny uttered a weary sigh and pulled his cell out of his pocket. His fingers shook as he tapped the contact for the woman he loved.

"What's wrong?" she asked the minute she picked up. She knew him so well.

"I think I just royally screwed up," he admitted.

He didn't have to worry that Teddie would think less of him for his mistake. Because she knew him, she knew that his heart was always in the right place—even if his head and his mouth were sometimes late to the party.

"I'm really worried about Cole."

"I saw the news," Teddie said. "They reported an incident at the Bentler estate, that two people were taken to the hospital."

He should have called her earlier. "I'm fine," he assured her.

"But Cole isn't?"

"No, he's fine." Physically. "All of the team is okay, and we didn't lose the person we're supposed to be protecting."

"That's good," she said. "But please be careful."

He heard the love in her voice, and it warmed his heart. He was so damn lucky that the woman of his dreams loved him as much as he loved her.

He could only wish that Cole could finally find the same happiness that he and their other friends had. But he was worried that Cole might not survive this assignment with his heart or his life.

Chapter 7

Cole could not see anything except that picture of Emery Little in his mind as he barreled out of the library. The guy's eyes had been dark, like Shawna's.

But, as Cole had already noticed, Maisy's were blue. He'd started getting suspicious then, but when Shawna had made the comment about her age, he'd brushed aside those suspicions. And he'd just assumed that Emery's eyes had probably been blue. But they hadn't been.

Wasn't it genetically impossible for two dark-eyed parents to have a blue-eyed baby? He couldn't remember his biology classes well enough to be certain of that. But he was certain that Maisy's eyes weren't just blue—they were the same blue as his. As his father's. As his grandfather's.

Her eyes were Bentler blue.

Because he wasn't looking where he was going, he didn't see her until he'd nearly bowled her over. Instinctively he reached out and caught her before she fell.

His mother clutched his arms to steady herself. Then she tried to smile at him through the tears streaming down her face. With her long blond hair and flawless complexion, she didn't look old enough to be his mother. Tiffani had been just a college intern at his father's business when his parents had met—a meeting she'd once drunkenly admitted to orchestrating. Drinking, which was something she used to do often, had always brought out her honesty, like how she'd decided in college that she'd rather marry money than earn it herself.

That honesty had cost her a relationship with Cole's father and with him. But while he didn't always respect her, he still cared about her.

"What's wrong?" he asked, concerned over her tears. "Has something happened?"

She shook her head. "Nothing since this morning," she said as she wiped at her face, smearing her usually perfect makeup. "It's been quite an emotional day."

"You were that close to Emery Little?" he asked.

"No," she replied. "Not at all. I'm talking about Shawna. How we nearly lost her."

Cole didn't have her. He'd given her up six years ago. Was that why she hadn't told him about Maisy? Had she been that angry with him over the breakup?

"And poor Astin," his mother continued. "It's so frightening that we nearly lost him, as well."

We. His father had died years ago but his mother continued to live with his grandfather even after she'd remarried. She continued to live off his grandfather.

Of course his father had left her nothing after learning that she'd gotten pregnant on purpose, that she'd done that just to trap him into their loveless marriage. His father had loved Cole, but he had never loved her. And he'd made that painfully clear to both of them when he'd left his entire estate to Cole.

His grandfather must have felt sorry for her because he let her and Jeff live with him. Of course what were a couple more when he had the entire rest of his family living off him?

He hadn't said anything aloud, and yet his mother reacted as if he'd spoken his thoughts.

She shuddered and dropped her hands from his arms. "You look so much like your father," she murmured. "Just as judgmental as he always was."

And now he felt even more regret for hurting her. Before he could reach out for her again, she whirled away and headed back down the hall toward the front stairwell. Where had she been going? Back to the library?

He never remembered her being much of a reader. But then maybe she'd been seeking out Manny for another conversation. She might have been one of the people who'd pointed out Maisy's resemblance to him.

He doubted she had anything beyond suspicion,

though. She wouldn't know for certain. Only Shawna would know for certain. And possibly one other person.

Cole couldn't risk talking to Shawna again—not so soon after he'd given into temptation and kissed her. It had been nothing, just a brush of his lips across hers. But it had shaken him to his core.

And he'd wanted more. He'd wanted to crawl into that bed with her and hold her like he used to—with nothing between them but the frantic pounding of their hearts. But that wasn't possible anymore.

There was too much between them. Too much heartbreak, too much resentment and too much loss. She hadn't even buried her husband yet. Or whatever she intended to do with his ashes...

Maybe she intended to keep them as a constant reminder of the man. Had he meant that much to her?

Not so much that she hadn't closed her eyes and welcomed Cole's kiss and leaned into it. He could have deepened it, could have ignited the passion that had always burned so hotly between them.

But she was vulnerable right now, and he couldn't confront her—not when he was so angry. No. There was only that one other person he could talk to now. The other person who might know...

He continued through the foyer but unlike his mother, he didn't climb the winding stairwell to the second story of the mansion. He crossed over the marble floor of the foyer to the double doors of the parlor and continued to the room that opened off it.

His grandfather's office. Cole knew he was there. His grandfather wasn't one of the elderly who needed naps. Even after his heart attack, he'd admitted that he struggled to rest. Sleep felt too much like death, he'd told Cole and his doctor. He would have plenty of time for sleep when he was dead.

Cole had a feeling he might not have to wait long. Smoke furled out from beneath the doors. He pushed them open to the smog and the sweet scent of his grandfather's expensive cigars.

Xavier jumped guiltily and dropped the stub into the glass of scotch he also held. "Damn it, boy, you scared me."

That was only fair since Cole was scared, too.

"You should have knocked," Xavier admonished him. But then he focused on Cole's face and drew in a shaky breath. "What's wrong now?"

"You tell me," Cole challenged him. "You tell me if Maisy is my daughter."

His grandfather leaned back in his big, leather chair and chuckled. "How the hell would I know that?"

"Because you know everything." At least that was the way it had always seemed to Cole, who'd always come to his idol for all the answers.

He hadn't consulted with Xavier before breaking his engagement, though. He knew his grandfather would have advised him against it. Since the first time she'd met Xavier as a little girl, he had always had a soft spot for Shawna, too.

Xavier sighed and shook his head. "If only I did." He thumped a fist on his desk, making the cigar jump up in the glass of scotch. "Then I'd know who the hell is trying to hurt our girl."

"Our girl?" That was what he'd always called

her—when Cole had first brought a young Shawna Rolfe home to play. "She's not our girl anymore."

"That's your own damn fault," Xavier said. "You broke it off with her."

"Was she pregnant when I did?" he asked.

Xavier shrugged. "I don't know, son. If she was, I could understand her not wanting to say anything to you—not with how your father felt about your mother." He shook his head and shuddered. "You're so much like him."

His mother had just said the same thing, but his grandfather's words struck him harder. "What do you mean?"

"He was stubborn," Xavier said. "And he, too, thought he was indestructible."

"I may have thought that once," Cole admitted. When he'd first joined the Marines, he'd been convinced nothing would happen to him. Then he'd had too many close calls and lost too many friends to count on anything. "But I learned the truth."

His grandfather studied his face for several long moments before nodding in silent agreement.

"And I want to learn the truth now," Cole said. "About Maisy. Is she mine?"

Xavier shrugged. "The only person who can answer that question for you is her mother. You need to talk to Shawna." His gaze narrowed and sharpened on Cole's face. "Why aren't you with her? You're supposed to be guarding her."

"Nikki Payne is protecting her and Maisy right now."

"Nikki? That little slip of a woman?" Xavier scoffed.

Cole was the one who chuckled now. "Don't let her hear you say that or she'll kick your ass. She's probably the best damn bodyguard Cooper has." Or Cole wouldn't have trusted her to protect Shawna and her daughter.

Or was Maisy *their* daughter?

"I don't care how damn good she is," Xavier said. "She's not you. You're the one who should be protecting Shawna and Maisy."

"Why?" Cole persisted. Because the little girl was his?

Xavier had to know, but his blue eyes were downcast, as if he was unwilling to meet Cole's gaze. "Because you're the best," he said.

And Cole laughed. Xavier had no way of knowing if that were true. He was new to this whole bodyguard business. "You don't know that."

"I know that you're the best person to protect them," Xavier clarified.

Fear struck Cole's heart. Was his grandfather trying to tell him without actually saying the words? Was he a father?

Panic gripped him at the thought. What the hell did he know about being a parent? About doing the right thing? He damn sure hadn't had very good examples of that in his life, not in his family at least. Yes, his father had married his mother when she'd gotten pregnant, but he'd never loved her. She probably hadn't ever loved him either, though.

And his grandfather had been married three times—to the mothers of each of his three sons. The first two marriages had ended in divorce, and he'd outlived the last wife. She passed away years ago.

His family wasn't good at marriage. Cole had been crazy to ever propose to Shawna in the first place. Bentlers weren't much better parents than they were marriage partners. His father had been so busy making money and living on the edge that he hadn't had much time for Cole. And Grandfather had enabled his children instead of making them self-sufficient.

At least Cole had his friends as examples. They did the right thing. Cooper had a happy marriage, and he was a parent. And a damn good one. But Coop had a good example in a mother that everyone in the Payne Protection family business considered theirs, whether she was biologically or not.

Whether Cole would be good at parenting didn't matter. What mattered was finding out the truth. Finding out if he actually was a father.

Maisy was in her mother's bedroom, in her mother's bed. He couldn't talk to Shawna now, in front of the little girl, even if he trusted himself to confront her when he was still so furious with her. He still hated himself for the things he'd said to her when he'd broken their engagement, and he'd done that to help her avoid pain.

But if he found out she'd kept his daughter from him…

He wasn't certain he would be able to protect her—from him and the things he might say. And even if she'd betrayed him that badly, he didn't want to hurt her anymore.

A chill chased over Shawna, rousing her awake with a shiver. She hadn't been sleeping very soundly, though. She couldn't shut off her mind, couldn't stop remembering all the horrible things that had been happening—to Emery, to Astin and to her.

And nearly to Cole.

What if she'd struck him with the car? He could have died never knowing that he was a father, that he had an amazing little girl. That *they* had an amazing little girl.

Where was Maisy?

Shawna felt around the tangled blankets, but she didn't find anyone else in her bed. The little warm body that had been burrowed against hers was gone. But that wasn't the only reason she'd suddenly gotten so cold.

The drapes rustled as a cold breeze blew through them. Needing fresh air despite all the oxygen she'd had at the hospital, she had opened a window earlier. But knowing how the temperature dropped at night, she'd only cracked it a tiny bit—not enough for the wind to be blowing the curtains like that. Why was it open so much wider?

She shivered and not just from the cold. Where was her daughter?

"Maisy?"

Had she gone back to her own bed? Usually it was the other way around. Maisy started out in her own bed and wound up in Shawna's. At least at home. They hadn't been staying with Xavier long enough to develop a pattern here. Maybe that was why the little girl had gotten confused.

Or maybe she'd just gotten up to use the bathroom. Shawna suspected that she'd had way too much to eat and drink throughout the day. Shawna had been too distracted to keep a good eye on her.

Of course she'd been preoccupied with the funeral and with nearly getting killed. If she hadn't been trapped in the garage, she would have done a better job watching her daughter. Usually she was a very good mother who would do anything to protect her daughter, even hide her paternity.

Shawna sat up and peered around the dark room. She couldn't see anything until the wind sifted through the drapes again and moonlight partially illuminated the room.

She gasped as she saw the shadow near the bed. It was too tall—too big—to be her little girl. But there was definitely someone else in her room.

"Cole?" she asked.

But she wasn't sure the person was big enough to be him. Cole was so broad. If it was him, he was taking this bodyguard thing too far if he felt as though he had to watch her sleep. "Cole?"

The shadow didn't answer her, didn't reveal his identity. Cole would have told her who he was.

Fear chilled her more than the wind, and her hand shook as she fumbled around for the lamp beside the bed. But before she could find the switch, a strong hand closed around her wrist.

A leather glove bit into her skin. And then something bit into her neck—a noose dropped over her head. She reached for it with her free hand, but before she could jerk it away, it tightened. The fibers bit into her throat.

She tried to scream, but her throat was already raw

from the carbon monoxide. And now it was choked as she fought for breath—as she fought for her life.

Nikki was pissed. It was going to happen.

She was going to get all maternal despite her best intentions. She should have known. She'd already fallen for Lars's nephew before she'd even known Blue was an Ecklund. Well, at least before she'd known for sure. She'd suspected, though. She'd actually thought he was Lars's kid.

She thought maybe that was why she fell for Blue because—she'd fallen for Lars despite all her best intentions. She glanced down at the diamond on her finger. She hadn't just fallen in love. She'd gotten engaged, was getting married.

And now—or at least someday—she was going to want kids. Because little Maisy Little was getting to her just like Blue had. Her tiny fingers wrapped tightly around Nikki's hand and around her heart. She needed to get back to her post outside Shawna's door.

Maisy had distracted her when she'd come out of the bedroom, looking all befuddled and sleepy. Still mostly asleep, she'd stared blankly up at Nikki.

Although she didn't babysit them much, Nikki had enough nieces and nephews to know little kids barely made it through the night without at least one bathroom break. So she'd brought her to the one next to Shawna's bedroom. After she'd done her business, though, the little girl hadn't wanted to go back to her mother's room; she'd wanted to go to her own.

So Nikki had brought her to the room that must have been recently redecorated. The pink paint smelled fresh and all the dainty furnishings looked brand-new, too. She'd tucked the little girl into the princess bed with its wispy pink canopy. But Maisy had grabbed her hand and wouldn't let go.

"You can go back to sleep now," Nikki assured her.

But those little blue eyes were wide open. They were the same deep blue as Cole's. She had to be his kid. Did he know? Suspect at least?

Those blue eyes widened more with fear.

"What's wrong?" Nikki asked her. Not that the kid hadn't been through a whole hell of a lot for a five-year-old. She'd lost the man she'd at least thought was her dad, whether he was or not. And she'd nearly lost her mom. Nikki squeezed her hand gently with reassurance.

"I saw a monster..." Maisy whispered, so softly that Nikki had to lean closer to hear her.

"A monster?" She must have had a bad dream. "Where was this monster?"

She couldn't lie to the kid and say there was no such thing as monsters. Nikki had met too many of them in her lifetime to convincingly sell that story. But she could look under the bed and in the closet and assure the little girl that none were in here.

But then Maisy whispered, "In Mommy's room. I saw the monster in Mommy's room."

And dread filled Nikki. She'd left her subject unprotected and alone with a monster.

Chapter 8

Cole couldn't wait until morning to find out the truth. He had already been in the dark for six years. And dark was how he found the hallway outside Shawna's room—dark and empty. Where the hell was Nikki?

While Lars was at the hospital with Astin, Manny patrolled the main floor and Cooper and Dane were on the outside perimeter, Nikki was supposed to be protecting Shawna. Maybe she'd gone inside the room. But when he tried the knob, he found the door locked. Nikki wouldn't have locked it.

Would she?

He knocked. "Hey, it's Cole, let me in!" He needed answers and not just about whether or not he was a father. He needed to know whether or not Shawna was safe.

Something clattered, then must have rolled to the floor and shattered. He could hear the tinkling of breaking glass inside the room. Then he heard something that scared him even more—a scream. It wasn't loud. It wasn't strong. But it was unmistakably Shawna's. She sounded weak, though. And even more scared than he was.

He stepped back, then hurled his body at the door. Wood splintered as the jamb broke and he fell into the room. Only a tiny pool of dim light from the hall penetrated the darkness inside but it was enough for him to see the dark shadow looming over the bed.

But he couldn't see enough to safely fire his weapon. He might hit Shawna or Maisy. So instead of drawing his gun, he hurled himself at that shadow. It moved as he did, and instead of knocking a body to the ground, he knocked the air from his own lungs as he hit the floor hard.

He didn't stay down. He rolled to his feet and pursued the shadow as it slipped through the drapes. Cole tore the fabric from the rod, jerking them aside. The shadow had slipped through the open window and onto the balcony that stretched the back of the entire house. Cole swung one leg over the windowsill to pursue the intruder before glancing back at the bed.

Shawna lay limply against the pillows, her face stark white in the moonlight. She wasn't unconscious like she'd been in the car after she'd crashed it through the garage door. Instead she was desperately clawing at the rope drawn tightly around her throat.

His heart slammed against his ribs as he rushed toward the bed. He pulled a knife from the sheath next to his holster. Careful of her throat, he sliced the blade through the thick rope.

She gasped for breath, drawing in deep gulps of it, as tears streamed from the corners of her eyes.

"Are you all right?" he asked. Her skin was so red and chafed from the coarse fibers of the rope.

She nodded, then she threw her arms around his neck, clinging to him as she trembled. Maybe it was in fear. Maybe it was from the cold wind sweeping through the room.

His arms wound around her, holding her tightly. "You're all right," he told her even though he wasn't convinced that she was. "You're safe now." She was nearly strangling him, as she clung to him.

He should have peeled her arms away, should have gone out the window after her attacker. But he needed to hold her as much as she needed to be held. He needed to assure himself that she was all right, that she was alive.

Because he'd nearly lost her...

If he hadn't come to see her when he had, he most certainly would have lost her. He trembled slightly with dread at the thought. Then he forced himself to pull back and ask, "Did you see who it was?"

She shook her head. "No," she said, her voice just a raspy whisper. "It was too dark until you pulled down the drapes and by then he was already gone."

It was probably painful for her to talk, with the way she sounded. But he had to know more details so he could stop this person. "He?"

"I don't know." She pushed him back and peered around the room. "Where's Maisy? When I fell asleep, she was here!" she exclaimed, her voice rising now as it cracked with panic. "Did he take her?"

"No," Cole assured her. The intruder wouldn't have been able to move so quickly if he or she had been carrying a child. "No." But then where was the little girl?

Before he could look for her, he heard a noise— one he knew too well. It was the metallic click of a gun cocking. He tensed, furious with himself now for dropping his guard.

But then a slightly husky yet feminine voice murmured, "Somehow I don't think you're the monster that Maisy saw."

Maisy saw the killer?

Shawna tensed and jerked herself out of Cole's arms. After her second close call with death, it had felt so good to be held, to be comforted.

But now she needed to be the one offering comfort. "Where is she?" she asked the curly-haired brunette who still held her gun on Cole. "Where's my daughter?"

But before the woman could reply, Cole whirled angrily toward her. "Nikki! Where the hell were you? An intruder nearly strangled Shawna to death." He held up the rope that he'd hacked off her throat.

"Oh, my God," the woman exclaimed. "I'm sorry I left my post. But when Maisy came out of the room, she didn't say anything about the monster...until I was tucking her in to her bed."

Shawna's heart lurched with fear for her daughter's safety. "She saw him! Where is she?"

"She's in her room with the door locked," Nikki said. "Manny's on his way up from the main floor and Cooper's coming in from the grounds."

Cole cursed. "He might miss the intruder."

"Dane's out there yet," Nikki said. Then she headed toward the window, her gun still drawn. She apologized again before she stepped over the sill and onto the porch.

But Shawna was relieved. She was glad Nikki had made certain that her child was safe before checking on her. But how safe was the little girl if she'd seen the attacker? Shawna threw back the covers and swung her legs over the side of the bed. But before she could step onto the floor, Cole jerked her back.

"There's glass over there," he warned her.

And in the moonlight, she could see the shards of the broken Tiffany lamp glittering against the hardwood floor. When he'd knocked on the door, she'd managed to knock over the lamp to alert him that she needed help. If he hadn't broken in the door when he had...

She shuddered, thinking of how close she had come to dying, to leaving her daughter without a mother.

Cole touched her neck. "It looks bad. You need to be taken to the hospital and checked out."

She shook her head. "I'm not going back there."

"But you could have broken bones—"

"Nothing's broken." She could move her neck. Her throat wasn't as sore from the rope as it was from the carbon monoxide. "It looks bad because my skin is so pale."

But because it looked bad, she couldn't have Maisy see her like this. The little girl was already afraid of the monster she had seen in Mommy's room. "You need to check on…" She nearly said it, nearly said, *our daughter.*

He needed to know in case the next time he wasn't able to save her. He needed to know so that if the killer was successful, Maisy wasn't all alone in the world.

Before Shawna could say anything, though, they heard knocking from the hallway—on Maisy's door, from the sound of it. And a deep voice called out gently, "It's okay to let me in. I'm not a monster."

Cole chuckled. "I'm not so sure about that."

Cole helped Shawna out of the bed on the other side, away from the glass, and he picked up her robe from the bench at the foot of the bed. "Here," he said. "Put this on and pull the collar around your neck."

He must have known that she needed to see her child. And Maisy needed to see her. They walked quickly to the little girl's room, where Manny was standing just outside. The minute Shawna called through the door, "It's Mommy, honey. You can open the door," the knob rattled, then turned and the door opened.

Maisy threw herself against Shawna, clinging to her. "I shouldn't have left you alone with the monster."

"I'm okay," Shawna assured her. "I'm okay."

Manny watched as Shawna dropped to her knees

and held her daughter closely. But he wasn't staring at her with the suspicion he'd shown earlier. Instead there was compassion in his dark eyes. "Monster?" He glanced at Cole then. "You?"

Cole shook his head. "I didn't get a good look at him." And he, too, got on his knees next to Maisy. His hand shook slightly as he patted her back. "Did you see the monster?"

The little girl lifted her head from Shawna's shoulder and peered at the man she had no idea was her father. But did Cole know?

Would he be shocked when she told him? Would he hate her like his father had hated his mother for getting pregnant? But Shawna hadn't done it purposely. She'd been using oral contraceptives for a while, but they weren't a hundred percent effective. And she and Cole had made love so many times that last night.

At least she'd made love. She wasn't sure what he'd been doing because it wasn't long after that he'd broken their engagement and her heart.

"Did you save Mommy from the monster?" Maisy asked Cole.

"Yes, he did," Shawna told her.

Maisy pulled away from her to throw her arms around Cole's neck. She clung to him like Shawna had after he'd cut that rope from around her throat.

"Thank you," she said. "Thank you for guarding Mommy from the monster!"

"That's my job," Cole said.

Was that the only reason he was so determined to protect her? To save her? Just because it was his job?

He stroked his hand over Maisy's hair. There was

still a slight tremor in it. "I will protect you, too," he assured the little girl.

And he sounded like he was doing more than just his job. He stared down at the child almost in wonder. Did he suspect that she was his? Or did he know?

"You can tell me what you saw," he urged their daughter.

Maisy's breath escaped in a shaky sigh, and her little brow furrowed. "I was sleeping," she said. "But I heard something. Then I saw the curtains moving." She shivered. "And I got out of bed and came into the hall." She turned back to Shawna and her eyes, which were already so deep a blue like her father's, filled with tears of regret. "I'm sorry, Mommy. I'm sorry I left you alone."

"You did the right thing," Shawna assured her. "You were very smart and very brave."

"The window was open?" Manny asked. And now his brow was furrowed with confusion. "We checked all the windows in your room earlier. We made sure they were locked."

Shawna's face heated with embarrassment over her stupidity. "I—I opened one a little bit after everyone had left. I needed some air." Despite all the oxygen she'd been given at the hospital, Shawna hadn't been able to fill her lungs deeply enough with fresh air. But she had selfishly put herself and her child at risk. "I'm sorry."

Cole reached out and squeezed her shoulder. "I understand."

"But you need to be more careful," Manny added. And now the judgment was back. The man really didn't seem to trust her at all. And with the way he was studying Cole and Maisy, it was clear he had his suspicions about the little girl's paternity.

Shawna wasn't about to admit the truth in front of him. Or in front of Maisy. But she needed to tell Cole.

Because no matter how determined he seemed to protect her life, the killer seemed just as determined to end it. And if she didn't survive, she needed to know that Maisy would not be alone in the world like she had been after she'd lost her parents. She needed to know that her little girl would have Cole, too—saving her from all the monsters in the world.

Cooper slid the library doors closed and focused on his team. At least the team members he'd gathered together. Lars had just arrived back from the hospital. The chauffeur had awakened again but didn't remember anything more than he had the first time Lars had spoken with him. So he was in no danger.

Shawna was the one in danger. And that was why Cole had insisted on staying by her side—her side and her daughter's side. But Cooper didn't want to leave him without backup for long.

"This is going to be a quick meeting," Cooper said. He prided himself that most of his meetings were quick. He wasn't like his brothers, Logan and Parker, who seemed to enjoy listening to themselves talk.

As a Marine, Cooper had always been given more to action—like his half brother Nick. When he wasn't able to act, he was given to frustration, which coursed through him now. He was pissed.

"So you guys didn't see any signs of the intruder running from the house?" Manny asked.

Cooper shook his head, and Dane, who'd been posted at the gates to the driveway, shook his head, as well.

Nikki glared at Manny. "Don't try to say it didn't happen. I saw the rope. And Cole saw someone jump out the window."

"The window she opened," Manny said.

"Can you blame her?" Nikki asked. "After being nearly burned alive a few months ago, you more than anyone should be able to understand her wanting some fresh air."

Manny cursed, either because he was remembering the assignment he nearly hadn't survived or because he was frustrated that Shawna was no longer a suspect. He groaned. "It's not her," he begrudgingly agreed. "But it still has to be someone in this house."

Cooper didn't like to jump to conclusions. "We don't know that for certain." But he definitely had his suspicions, as well. "Someone could have come inside from the outside. As you stated, she had the window open."

"But then where did they go?" Nikki asked. "I went out that window after him and didn't see anything."

"But me," Cooper reminded her of how she'd run into him shortly after she'd climbed down the balcony from the second story.

Good thing she didn't shoot as quickly as she used to, or she might have fired at him—like she'd fired at their brother Nick a few times. Of course none of them was certain that had been an accident. She'd had her issues with Nick. Now they were the closest of the siblings, so close that she'd been the best man at Nick's wedding.

"And you didn't see anyone?" Manny asked Cooper.

He shook his head again. "No."

"Then whoever went out that window must have gone back inside the house," Manny said. "And I was upstairs checking on the little girl, so I didn't see who might have come inside through a door downstairs."

"Whoever it is could have also come back into the house through another open window off the second story balcony," Nikki said.

"One that he or she might have left open," Manny added. And he cursed again. "It's one of Cole's family."

"You would rather it was Shawna?" Nikki asked him.

Manny didn't deny it. Instead he replied, "Cole would probably be safer if it was."

And they all stared at him. Nikki, of course, was the one who asked, "Why?"

"Because then he wouldn't trust her."

"He already doesn't," Cooper said. "He didn't even want to take this case."

And maybe Cooper shouldn't have forced him to because now there was no way his friend wasn't going to get hurt—emotionally. And probably physically, as well.

Chapter 9

While the immediate threat of danger was gone—
out the window into the night—Cole's heart pounded
frantically as fear still overwhelmed him. He was
more afraid of this—the little girl and her mother—
than he had been of any of his previous missions.

They posed the greatest danger to him.

"I looked under your bed and in the closet and in
the bathroom," Cole said. He had his weapon drawn,
but the safety was on. He wasn't going to risk any
chance of it accidentally misfiring around Maisy. "I
can vouch that there are no monsters in here."

Maisy expelled a shaky little sigh and leaned back
against her pillows. Her lids seemed so heavy that she
could barely keep them open, but she blinked furi-

ously, as if fighting sleep. Her thick black lashes fluttered, as she lifted her lids and focused on his face.

Shawna knelt next to the bed, beneath the pink canopy, her hand over her daughter's on the edge of the pink blankets. "There is no such thing as monsters," she told the little girl. She looked up at Cole, as if beseeching him to back up her claim.

But he would not lie to the child. He knew there were indeed such things as monsters. During his missions, as a bodyguard and a Marine, he had encountered too many to deny their existence.

"But—but what about the one I saw in your room?" Maisy asked, her eyes widening now with fear as she remembered what she'd seen.

"It was just the wind blowing through the curtains," Shawna replied.

Cole felt a pang in his heart over how easily she lied. Would she tell him the truth—if he asked her directly—who the little girl's father really was? Could he believe whatever she told him? Or would he need to demand a paternity test in order to know for certain?

"Cole…" Maisy sleepily murmured his name. Apparently she, too, was waiting for him to back up her mother's claim that there were no monsters.

He holstered his weapon and knelt beside her bed on the opposite side from Shawna. He couldn't be close to her right now. Every time he was, he wound up holding her, so he couldn't trust himself not to do it again. He couldn't hold her, couldn't get close to her, when he couldn't trust her.

"Yes, Maisy?" he asked the child. If she asked him

outright if there were monsters, he wouldn't lie to her. So he hoped that wasn't what she wanted to ask him.

"Can you kiss me good-night?" she asked.

That question struck him harder than anything else she might have asked him. The vise gripped his heart tightly, squeezing it so that it stopped pounding for a second before resuming at a frantic pace. He leaned forward and brushed his lips across her forehead.

Maisy closed her eyes and settled into her pillows with a whisper-soft sigh. And something else flooded his chest: love.

Cole had fallen for her. Just like that.

Just as quickly and hard as he'd fallen for her mother all those years ago. He closed his eyes for a moment to deal with all the emotions flooding him. Despite how furious he would be at Shawna if she'd kept his daughter from him, he wanted Maisy to be his. He wanted to be her father.

He had to know. But when he opened his eyes again, he found only the child in the room.

Shawna was gone.

Shawna wanted to run. But she didn't know where to flee. She didn't know where she would be safe or whom she could trust. After nearly being strangled to death in her room, she hesitated outside the door. The jamb was splintered from where Cole had kicked it open.

If he hadn't…

She shuddered with the certainty that she would be dead. She wouldn't have been able to fight off her attacker any longer.

Then her little girl would have thought she was an orphan and all alone like Shawna had once been. Shawna needed to tell not just Cole but Maisy, too, the truth. That they had each other.

The fear of them both hating her was what she wanted to run from now. She couldn't handle Cole looking at her the way his father had looked at his mother—with contempt. And while Maisy was too sweet to ever hate anyone, she would be confused and hurt to learn that Shawna had lied to her. Her trust in her mother would be irrevocably shattered.

After that, would they ever be able to have the relationship they'd once had? Would Shawna have damaged it beyond repair?

Strong hands gripped her shoulders, and a gasp of fear and surprise slipped through her lips. But then she recognized that touch, as her skin began to tingle. She didn't have to fear physical harm. Cole would never hurt her that way, no matter how angry he got when she told him the truth.

And she had to tell him the truth.

She had already waited six years too long. She couldn't wait another moment, especially with someone so determined to kill her.

But before she could say anything, Cole turned her away from her bedroom door and steered her down the hall. "It's not safe for you to stay in that room," he told her. "Not until the door and the jamb get repaired." He removed one hand from her shoulder to open another door and escorted her inside.

"Whose room is this?" she asked as she noticed

the suitcase lying on the bench at the foot of the bed. "I can't just take someone else's room."

"It's mine," he told her. "All of the bodyguards have rooms near yours and Maisy's."

"Maisy," she said. "Is she safe?" She shouldn't have left her little girl alone and unprotected. But as she glanced back toward the hall, she saw Nikki passing by.

"She will be very safe," Cole assured her. "Nikki won't let anything happen to her."

She trusted the female bodyguard, which slightly eased the burden of concern for her daughter's safety.

It was time to ease another of those burdens. It was time to tell Cole the truth. She pushed the door to his room closed and turned back toward him. He was so damn handsome even with dark circles of fatigue rimming his deep blue eyes. It was late, and it had already been a long day for him.

A long day of saving her from danger...

"Thank you," she said. She had not been very gracious when he'd first showed up at the funeral and the memorial brunch. And she'd been so terrified over the intruder nearly strangling her and so afraid for Maisy that she couldn't remember if she had thanked him or not.

But he shrugged off her gratitude. "You shouldn't have been in that situation. We should have protected you better."

"I shouldn't need protection," she said. And she had no idea why she would. Why in the world would someone want *her* dead?

"You didn't recognize anything about your attacker?" he asked. "Size? Smell? Did he say anything?"

She shook her head. "I'm not even sure it was a man. I was lying in bed, so I have no idea how tall the person is. And I didn't smell anything." The carbon monoxide had probably affected her sense of smell, though.

"Damn it," he murmured, and a muscle twitched along his tightly clenched jaw. "There was nothing at all familiar about the attacker?"

"No, but it's obvious you think I should have recognized him," she said. "You really think it could be one of them? Of your family?" From the tension on his face and in his voice, it was clearly tearing him up inside to suspect one of them of being a killer.

"It has to be," he said.

She wasn't as convinced. While she wasn't a fan of his cousins and uncles, she couldn't see any of them being ruthless enough to kill someone. "Why?"

"Access," he said. "It has to be someone staying inside this house. That's why no one has noticed anyone being where they shouldn't be—like when your laptop was left in the library."

She felt obligated to point out, "Family are not the only people in this house." She was not family. Unfortunately her daughter was.

His brow furrowed with his confusion. "Who are you talking about? My friends?"

They were *his* friends. If they all considered her marrying Emery to be a betrayal of Cole, they also had a motive for wanting to kill her.

"Manny certainly doesn't like me."

He snorted. "He's loyal."

She tensed. "And I'm not?" She had been faithful to him since she'd met him. When he'd left for boot camp and his deployments, she'd never considered dating anyone else even though she'd been asked.

He arched a brow. "You must have already known Emery to have married him as quickly as you did."

"We met at the high school while I was helping coach the cheerleaders and he worked with the marching band," she said. But there had never been an attraction between them. Ten years older than she was, he'd always been more like an overprotective big brother than a potential lover.

"I don't remember you ever talking about him," Cole said, and now there was suspicion in his voice.

Did he think she had been having an affair with Emery while they'd been engaged?

"He was a friend," she said. "Just a friend." Even after they'd married. She needed to tell Cole that, so he would realize that Maisy was his. But would he even believe her?

Her heart pounded frantically as she worried about his reaction. She was nearly as afraid as she'd been when she'd been locked in the garage, or when the noose had wrapped so tightly around her neck. Feeling as if she was being strangled again, she lifted her fingers to her throat.

Cole's fingers covered hers, pushing aside the collar of her robe.

He sucked in a sharp breath as he studied her neck. Then he said, "I should have brought you to the hospital."

"I'm a nurse," she reminded him—and herself. Her job was to take care of others, not to have them take care of her. But then, usually members of the medical profession made the worst patients. "I would know if I needed treatment."

"It's already beginning to bruise," he told her, as he stroked his fingers across hers and then along her throat.

Her skin tingled from his touch. "Nothing's broken," she said. Except her heart, which had been broken for the past six years. Not even the birth of her beautiful baby had mended the wound Cole had inflicted on her.

"My friends wouldn't have done this to you," he assured her. "And they certainly wouldn't have set the bomb in your vehicle. They were thousands of miles away in River City when your car blew up. It has to be someone else in this house, some member of my family."

"Why?" she asked. "What possible motive would anyone have to kill me?" Nobody knew, at least not for certain, that Maisy was a Bentler. And even if somebody knew, that would make Maisy the target—not Shawna.

Of course, once she told him the truth, she would understand if he didn't care what happened to her. He would never be able to get back the almost six years he had missed of his daughter's life. Guilt nearly overwhelmed her. No matter how angry and hurt Shawna had been, she never should have kept the truth from him. She never should have kept Maisy from him.

He shrugged. "I don't know what the motive is."

"I am not a threat to anyone's inheritance," she pointed out. Maisy would have been if anyone knew the truth about her paternity. So maybe she hadn't done such a bad thing when she'd kept her paternity secret. And maybe it was better, especially now, for no one to learn the truth. She couldn't risk putting Maisy in danger, too.

His blue eyes—so like their daughter's— narrowed as he studied her face. "No, *you're* not."

He must have begun to suspect that Maisy was his. And while revealing her paternity might put the child more at risk, her father and his friends would be even more motivated to protect the little girl and find out who was after Shawna.

Tears of frustration burned her eyes, and pain gripped her heart. Knowing that someone hated her enough to want her dead made her physically ill. The thought of Cole coming to hate her just as much made her feel even sicker, so that she just couldn't bring herself to tell him the truth. "So why?" she asked instead. "Why is someone so determined to kill me?"

His fingers skimmed up from her throat to her cheek. "We'll figure it out," he assured her.

She believed him. She only hoped that it wasn't too late to save her when they did. It was already too late to save her heart. She was falling for Cole all over again, just like she'd done all those years ago.

"Cole…" She murmured his name as she linked her arms around his neck.

He lowered his head until his mouth brushed across hers. It probably would have been a kiss like the one he'd given her a couple hours ago…if she hadn't opened her mouth, if she hadn't brushed her tongue across his lips.

If he hadn't groaned and deepened the kiss.

Passion ignited, burning hotly inside her. She knew once she told him the truth that he might not want her like she wanted him. That she might never get this chance again.

So she didn't stop him when he lifted and carried her the few feet away to the bed. And when he laid her down, she pulled him down with her—on top of her. And she welcomed the weight of his muscular body.

But it wasn't enough. She wanted him inside her, filling her like he once had. Maybe it was coming so close to dying that had her desperate to experience the pleasure she'd only felt with Cole. Or maybe it was just Cole—being near him again—that made her desperate.

Desperate times called for desperate measures. The plan—that had been so well thought out—had to be scrapped. There was no way to make Little's and Shawna's deaths look like a murder-suicide now.

Thanks to Cole.

Damn him!

What had he seen when he'd broken down that bedroom door? Had there been enough light from the hall to reveal the identity of the person who'd had the noose around Shawna's neck?

She'd been gasping for breath, nearly blacked out. So she hadn't seen anything. She'd been so close to death.

So close…

Her murder had nearly gone according to plan. Once she'd passed out, she would have been strung up from the railing of the balcony just outside her bedroom window. It would have looked like a suicide.

But Cole had ruined that when he'd rushed to her rescue, just like he always had. When would he learn to stop playing her white knight?

What had he seen?

Not enough or he would have been knocking down this bedroom door just like he had hers. No. Cole hadn't seen anything. He didn't know anything. And he wouldn't have time to figure anything out—because now Cole had to die.

The only way to get to Shawna would be to kill Cole first. And that would be no problem at all.

The ex-Marine bodyguard would never see it coming.

Chapter 10

Whatthe hell was he thinking?

He wasn't. That was the problem. Whenever Cole got close to Shawna, he couldn't think at all. He could only feel. The attraction, the desire… It burned inside him, so hot, so desperate.

He'd spent the past six years missing her, aching for her.

He needed to be with her, inside her. He needed to be part of her. So that he wouldn't crush her, he levered himself up on an arm and a knee, keeping the majority of his weight from settling on top of her slight body.

But she arched up from the mattress and clung to him, her lips moving hungrily over his. He deepened the kiss, and she eagerly welcomed his tongue sliding inside her mouth. Her hips pushed against the erection straining the fly of his black dress pants. Even through the material of his pants and her robe, he felt her heat. She was every bit as desperate for him as he was for her. He couldn't believe it.

And it was that doubt that began to clear the passion clouding his brain and overtaking his body. He pulled back, opened his eyes and stared down at her.

Her usually pale skin was flushed now with desire. Her dark eyes were even darker as she opened them and stared up into his face. Her brow furrowed with confusion, she blinked. And some of the passion cleared, leaving mostly fear.

The bruises on her throat were a painful reminder that she had every reason to be afraid. But she looked almost as afraid of him as she was of what could happen to her. Was she afraid that he was going to stop? Or did she have another reason to fear him?

Then he tensed as he realized what the reason could be: Maisy. Was she afraid that he might learn the truth and try to take his daughter away from her? Was that why she'd wound her arms around his neck? To distract him? If so, mission accomplished.

He was distracted. Even now, his body was tense and achy for hers. His erection throbbed, and his pulse pounded erratically. He found it difficult to even draw a breath. Although it wasn't just passion he felt now, but panic, as well.

He couldn't fall for her again. He couldn't love a woman he couldn't trust.

"What is this?" he asked, and he was surprised his voice didn't shake with how hard his heart was beating. "You haven't even buried your husband yet." His ashes still sat in that urn, abandoned in the library. Had she forgotten all about him? "Are you using me to replace him?" he wondered. "Or did you use him to replace me?"

She struggled beneath him, trying to buck him off. He knew, though, that if he let her up, she would run out of the room and probably straight into danger again. Just as she had the last time, when she'd run from the library into the garage where she'd been trapped.

Knowing how much danger she was in, he shouldn't have provoked her. But her passion had provoked him. How could she have married another man so soon after their breakup if she'd really loved him? Or had she had another reason for her quickie marriage? He had to know.

So he asked again, "Which is it, Shawna?"

Which of them was the man she really loved? Him or Emery? That was the question he really wanted to ask, but he didn't quite dare. He wasn't certain he could handle her answer.

Shawna was afraid. Not because of how Cole was holding her. She knew that he wouldn't hurt her. Physically. His grip on her wrist was light enough that she was able to tug free. He also let her up so that she could scoot out from under him on the bed.

She was afraid that the moment had come to tell the truth. And she wasn't certain how he would react. She wasn't convinced that he wouldn't hurt her emotionally. He was not the man she remembered, the man she'd loved. Something had changed him, had made him harder and more cynical. Had war done that?

Or had she?

She hadn't realized how he would react to her marrying another man. After the way he'd broken up with her, she hadn't thought he would even care. He'd seemed to want her out of his life for good then.

He had already changed then—six years ago—into a man she hadn't recognized. He'd grown more distant and colder, so cold that he had had no problem breaking their engagement and her heart.

No. She hadn't changed him. He'd already been changed because the man she'd known wouldn't have been able to hurt her like that.

"Why does it bother you?" she asked.

He snorted. "Wouldn't it bother you if you thought I was just using you to replace some other woman?"

Was he?

She knew why she wanted him. Despite her best efforts to get over him, she still loved him. What had been his excuse for kissing her back, for bringing her to the bed?

She had no doubt that he'd wanted her every bit as much as she'd wanted him. She'd felt his erection, had felt his heat and his passion. Her body ached still with need for his. If only he hadn't stopped...

"What if it was the other way around?" she asked.

His brow furrowed with his confusion. "What? I wasn't using you."

"What if I had used Emery?" she asked.

He tensed now. And she saw the realization on his face. He knew…

He already knew.

But that didn't mean she didn't have to confirm it. She owed him the truth, the whole truth, but she didn't know how much of it her pride would allow her to admit. He'd hurt her so badly. Her pride—and her daughter—were all she had left. But when he learned the truth about Maisy, would he be angry enough to try to keep her from her daughter?

"Then I'd feel even sorrier for him than I already do," Cole replied.

She flinched. Why did he pity her husband so much? Because he had died? Or because he'd married *her*? How could he think so little of her?

"He knew," she said.

Cole's blue eyes narrowed, and he focused intensely on her face. That muscle twitched again along his tightly clenched jaw.

A lump of emotion rose up in her sore throat, threatening to choke her more than that noose nearly had. But she swallowed it down and spoke clearly and succinctly. "Emery knew that I was pregnant when he married me," she said. "That's why he proposed."

"Did he know…?" Cole trailed off. "Is she…?"

He obviously couldn't bring himself to ask the question burning in his eyes. But she answered it anyway. "Yes, he knew the baby was yours."

Cole expelled a breath, like he'd been holding it and she'd sucker-punched him. And maybe she had. But she could see that he'd already begun to suspect the truth. Maisy would have her father.

If he wanted her…

Did he want her?

He looked too shocked for Shawna to determine what he was thinking. Or feeling. If anything at all, except confusion. "Why would he propose when he knew the baby was mine?"

Did Cole not believe her? Did he think she was lying about Maisy's paternity? "Because he was a good friend," Shawna said.

"He loved you."

He had. But just as a friend. She could have told him that, too. But she wasn't certain, after the things he'd said to her, that she wanted him to know she'd had only a platonic marriage. No passion. No sex. Only friendship. "He loved Maisy, too," she said. "He was a good father to her."

"To my daughter?"

Was he claiming the little girl or again just questioning Shawna's veracity? "Emery was a good man," she said. He hadn't deserved what happened to him. He'd been so happy, so hopeful, for the first time since he'd asked her to marry him. "He didn't want me to raise my daughter alone."

But she would have, since the alternative had been telling Cole the truth. She had been insistent that she wouldn't do that, even though Emery had encouraged her to come clean with him. He'd thought it might have made a difference, might have had Cole coming back to her. But she hadn't wanted him coming back because of the baby; she'd wanted him to come back because he loved her.

"Why didn't you tell me?" he asked.

"I didn't realize that I was pregnant until after you had already broken up with me," she said. And it had taken her a while to realize that she hadn't just been heartsick; she'd been morning sick, which unfortunately had pretty much lasted all day long.

"So you were angry?" he asked. "Vengeful?"

"Of course I was angry," she said. He had shattered her heart into a million irreparable pieces. She hadn't been spiteful, though. She'd been too broken for spite. "But that isn't why I didn't tell you."

She hadn't wanted him to hate her any more than he'd already seemed to when he had coldly ended their engagement. But she realized now that she had probably only delayed the inevitable because he was definitely looking at her as if he hated her now.

"Why not then?" he asked.

She wanted to explain that she'd thought she was doing what was best for everyone. But before she could say anything more, he jumped up from the bed.

He shook his head and expelled a shaky breath. "Never mind," he said. "I don't need to know."

What? Before Shawna could ask, he headed toward the door, opened it and stepped out into the hall.

Did it make no difference to him that Maisy was his? Did he not want their little girl?

That was another reason she hadn't told him the truth six years ago. She hadn't wanted him to reject their baby like he had rejected her. She had wanted her baby only to know love—not resentment or anger.

For a while it had worked—until that car had exploded. Now Maisy knew tragedy and loss and pain and fear. And Shawna knew failure, as a mother. She hadn't been able to protect her child from pain.

Would Cole? Or did he want nothing to do with her?

For the first time since his heart attack a few months ago, Xavier Bentler felt old. His bones ached with age and probably arthritis while his mind ached with frustration. He'd messed up. He shoved the cigar back into the glass of scotch he'd abandoned on his desk.

He'd screwed up badly.

And as usual, Cooper Payne had no compunction against pointing that out to him. He really would like to meet the woman who'd raised such a man. But hell, she would be too young for him. Now, maybe if Payne had a grandmother alive…

No. Xavier had long since given up on having a happy ending of his own. He'd lost out on that opportunity decades ago. But he'd wanted his grandson to have the chance to have a true and lasting love. There had been too damn little of that in the Bentler family.

"You really want to remove Cole from this assignment?" he asked Payne.

He nodded. "I think it's the only way to keep him safe."

"What about Shawna?" Xavier asked. After three attempts on her life, it was indisputable that she was the one in danger. But if Cooper was right, she wasn't the only one.

"The rest of my team will keep her safe," Payne assured him.

"What about Cole?" Xavier asked with concern

for his stubborn grandson. But that fierce obstinacy and independence was why Cole was his favorite. "Won't he be furious?"

Cole might not have wanted to come home, but now that he'd arrived, he seemed intent on protecting Shawna. Xavier couldn't imagine that he would take kindly to be removed from the assignment.

The door to his den flew open, and he had his answer. Cole was clearly furious. So much so he barely noticed that Payne had automatically drawn his weapon on him.

Cooper must have seen the fury, too, because he didn't immediately reholster the gun. "What's wrong?" he asked. "Has something happened? Has there been another attempt?"

Cole didn't even look at his boss. He just shook his head.

"If you're pissed because I put Manny on her protection duty—"

Cole held up his hand, palm out, toward Payne. "I'm not pissed at you," he said.

"He's mad at me," Xavier said. And he knew why. Because he knew...

Payne glanced back and forth between them, as if trying to figure out what the old man had done now. Xavier knew it was because he'd done nothing. He'd said nothing.

"How could you?" Cole demanded.

Xavier shrugged. "Depends on what we're talking about."

"You manipulative old bastard!" Cole said, his blue eyes hard with fury.

Xavier couldn't deny it. He'd done his share of manipulating his family over the years. But he'd refrained from messing with Cole. Until now. That was why he'd waited so long to step in. But the heart attack had given him no choice. He'd had to act soon. His patience and his life were running out.

Once Cole learned what else he'd done, he would be even more furious with him. And with damn good reason.

Chapter 11

Cole barely noted the closing of the door as Cooper left the den. His friend was astute—so astute that he must have realized Cole's argument with his grandfather was personal. This wasn't about the assignment. It wasn't about protecting Shawna at all. Or was it?

"Why didn't you tell me?" Cole asked.

"You had already left for that last deployment when she found out she was pregnant," his grandfather replied. "What was she supposed to do—send you a card with a picture of a stork on it? And a little note saying you're going to be a daddy? But she couldn't do that because nobody knew where the hell you were."

Half the time, neither had Cole. "Nobody could know."

His grandfather nodded. A veteran himself, Xavier had to understand. But even if he had, he still had betrayed Cole.

"I came back from that mission, though," Cole said. He'd been surprised that he had, that they had all survived. But then he'd been even more surprised when he'd learned Shawna had married another man. "You could have told me then."

"You weren't back long before you left for another," Xavier reminded him. "And another."

Each mission had been more dangerous than the last. But they'd survived them. Cole wasn't certain he could survive this, though. His heart was beating so hard, pounding away in his chest, that he felt battered from the inside out. "I lost five years of her life."

"Nearly six," Xavier said. "Her birthday is just a few weeks away."

So she acted older because she was older. Shawna had misled him about her age. And his grandfather had misled him about everything. Those betrayals struck him harder than any blow could have. He had never felt as devastated as he felt right now.

His legs began to shake, threatening to fold beneath him, so he dropped onto the chair Cooper had vacated moments ago. He was glad that he'd insisted his friends come home with him. Not that he'd ever really considered this place home. All the more reason he needed his friends. He needed people he could trust. This assignment was far more dangerous than he'd even realized.

"I can't believe you kept this from me all these years."

Xavier shrugged, as if trying to shake off the guilt he should be feeling. But Cole wasn't certain that he was. "She never told me for certain."

"But you knew," Cole called him on it before he could utter a lie.

His grandfather had always been an honest man—if not always a very open one. "Of course I knew. She has your eyes." He lifted his hand to his face. "My eyes. Your father's. You should have known the moment you saw her."

"She's a Bentler," Cole said. "So why wouldn't you claim her?"

"She's a Bentler," Grandfather said with a heavy sigh. "Maybe it's safer for her not to be."

He knew what Cole had already realized. Whoever was after Shawna was a member of their family. And if that person—that monster—realized that Maisy was a member of their family...

He shuddered at the thought of the little girl being in danger. "You're right. Nobody can know the truth."

He wasn't entirely sure he should have learned it because he had no idea what to do with the knowledge now. Did he act like a father to Maisy? But then everyone would know the truth. It wasn't safe for her to be a Bentler. Hell, it wasn't safe for her to be a Little right now either.

"Why did he do it?" Cole asked.

"What? Who?" his grandfather looked up at him, and it was apparent that he was tired. And old. Where had the manipulative bastard gone? The brilliant businessman who'd built a billion-dollar enterprise?

"Emery Little," Cole said. "Why did he claim Maisy as his?"

Xavier shrugged. "Why does any man do what he does?"

For love. He must have loved Shawna a lot, just like Cole had. He had loved her so much that he'd been willing to do what he'd thought was right to protect her. Cole uttered a ragged sigh.

"So I hope you'll understand that's why I changed my will," Xavier said.

"What?" Cole grimaced as he had a horrible premonition. "No." He'd already suffered the consequences of the last time a Bentler had changed his will. Sure, he was richer than he'd ever imagined he would be, but he was also more reviled.

His grandfather reached his hands across his desk, as if imploring him to understand. "Cole…"

But Cole just shook his head as the horror crept in. "You didn't."

"You and Shawna belong together," Grandfather said. "You have loved her since you were kids."

Cole shook his head. "That was puppy love," he said. "It wasn't real." Or she wouldn't have married Emery Little so soon after he broke their engagement. "We both outgrew it."

"Your father never outgrew his first crush," Xavier said.

Cole snorted. "What? You trying to tell me he loved my mother?"

"No," Xavier said. "And Natalie Montoya is why he couldn't."

Cole had never heard the name before. "Who was that?"

"His high school girlfriend," Xavier said.

"What happened?" Cole asked, curious despite all the turmoil going on inside him. "Did she marry another man?" A man like Emery Little?

Xavier uttered a very weary-sounding sigh and reached for his glass of scotch with a slightly trembling hand. "She died."

Cole gasped, thinking of how close he had come to losing Shawna. If she hadn't broken that car window and driven the vehicle through the carbon monoxide–filled garage... If he hadn't cut that noose from around her throat...

"That's terrible," he said. "Is that why Dad never mentioned her?"

Xavier leaned back in his chair, and his shoulders slumped. "Probably. Because what's worse than her dying is that your father caused her death."

Cole tensed. "What? What happened?"

"He was driving too fast." Grandfather sighed again, and it was the sigh of a broken man. "He was always driving too fast."

Cole had never considered his father to be the daredevil his grandfather did. He'd always just figured the guy was in a hurry—to make money, to be even more successful than his father. He hadn't driven fast just to drive fast but because he was driven.

"He lost control and hit a tree," Xavier said. "He walked away without a scratch. Physically. But he never got over her, just like you will never get over Shawna."

Cole shook his head. "It's not the same at all. And what you're describing with my father sounds more like guilt than love."

"You never felt guilty?" Xavier asked him. "You broke her heart when you broke your engagement with her. That never bothered you?"

Cole had felt guilty for things he'd said, for the way he'd hurt her. And if Shawna had died like his father's girlfriend had, he would have been broken, too. Broken beyond repair. "I did feel bad," he admitted wearily. "Until I found out she married Emery Little."

"You asked why he did it," Xavier said. "You didn't ask why *she* married him."

Cole furrowed his brow, trying to figure out what his grandfather was up to now. Although he already knew his end game in all of this was getting Cole back together with Shawna. And that could not happen for so many reasons.

"I don't care," Cole lied. "I don't care why she married him. The only thing I care about is keeping her safe until we figure out who the hell killed Little and keeps trying to kill her."

"Not we," said another voice.

Cooper had slipped back into the den without Cole even noticing. It probably didn't look good for the boss to see that his bodyguard skills had slipped so much. But he was preoccupied. And tired.

And shocked.

And a father…

"What do you mean, not we?" Cole asked. But he had a horrible feeling that he knew exactly what it meant and it wasn't that Cooper was quitting the job.

No matter how terrible their client, the Payne Protection Agency kept their promise to protect them.

"You're off this assignment," Cooper said, confirming Cole's suspicion. "I'm sending you back to River City."

"Hell no." That wasn't possible. While he had no intention of falling for Shawna again, he had every intention of keeping her alive. And Maisy.

He wasn't certain how to be a father. But he knew he'd have to try. For her.

As an ER nurse, Shawna had seen more people experiencing panic attacks than heart attacks, so she recognized her symptoms. The palpitations, the sweats, the short breaths.

She needed air. But as soon as she reached for the window, the door opened. She expected Cole to step back inside, so her heart raced even more. But it was Manny.

He looked all judgmental again. He must have heard. Or maybe Cole had talked to him, had told him about her latest betrayal. Or her six-year-long betrayal...

And she had no idea what to do about it. How to fix it. How to make Cole stop hating her. Because she knew that he did. She'd seen it on his face. The pain of him looking at her that way had her heart pounding and her lungs aching for air.

"I need to go outside," she said. "I need air." And whatever blew through the window would not be enough.

Manny shook his head. "It's too dangerous."

Tears began to sting her eyes. "I need air," she said, her voice cracking with the panic overwhelming her. "Or I'm going to lose it. I need to go outside and clear my head."

"I don't think it's your head you want to clear," he remarked.

She groaned. Sure, she wanted to clear her conscience. But she wasn't about to admit that to him. There was nothing she could do about that anyway. She couldn't give Maisy and Cole back the nearly six years she'd stolen from them. If only she could.

Manny murmured a curse, then acquiesced, "Okay. But I'm sticking close to you. And letting Dane know, so he's close, too."

She nodded. But she doubted the air would help with Cole's friends standing around her, judging her. And once they had gone down the back stairwell, through the kitchen, to the outside, she told him so. "Please."

"How many near-death experiences do you have to have before you realize you're in danger?" Manny asked.

Tears stung her eyes again, but she blinked them back. She was definitely going to shed them, but she wanted privacy for that. She wasn't going to look like a damsel in distress when she could help it. The noose around her neck—she hadn't been able to help that.

But crying, that she could control. But not for much longer.

"I know I'm in danger," Shawna said. "That's why I need to get some air."

Manny's dark eyes narrowed in skepticism. "I don't think that's your reason."

She wanted to curse at him. She wanted to release all her frustration and anger and vent it on Manny. But he was protecting her, and she owed him her gratitude.

"Please," she murmured again. "I will stay where you can see me. I just need to walk a little farther away from this house." She gestured toward the flower arbor just beyond the patio. The lights from the mansion illuminated the cobbled brick patio. But the arbor was beyond that, just within the shadows, to give her the privacy she needed to let her tears go. They were burning the back of her throat and her eyes.

Her bodyguard shook his head in refusal. "It's not safe."

She pointed toward his holster. He already had his hand on his weapon, and they hadn't moved a foot away from the house yet. "Can't you shoot that far?"

His mouth slid into a smirk. "I can shoot that far."

He was the one who'd taken the most to the sniper training. Shawna remembered that from Cole's letters. Before he'd broken up with her, he had written to her often. She felt like she knew his friends from everything he'd told her about them. She'd thought one day, when they were all back from their deployments and she and Cole were married, that they would become her friends, too.

She doubted that would ever happen now. If they hadn't already hated her, they were certain to after they learned that Maisy was Cole's daughter.

"Then I'm not in any danger," she pointed out. "If someone jumps out at me, you will shoot them."

He sighed. But he didn't stop her as she began to walk away. She stopped herself and turned back. "Unless it's Cole," she said. "Don't shoot Cole."

He fought it. She could see the struggle in the muscles of his face. Then he gave up the battle and let the smirk curve up his lips again. "My job is to protect *you*," he said. "And I take my job very seriously."

He was teasing about shooting Cole. They both knew he wouldn't hurt her. She'd be almost happy if he would try, though. She wished she'd gotten some reaction from him other than that cold silence when he'd just walked out of the bedroom.

Where had he gone? Had he left the estate? Had he left the state entirely? Had he returned to River City, Michigan?

She hoped he had. For his sake and for hers.

But not for Maisy. Her little girl had already lost her stepfather. She needed her father now. If something happened to Shawna, he might be all that she had.

Manny wanted to hate her. Out of loyalty to Cole, he wanted to hate her. But it was clear that Shawna was a good mother. She loved her daughter more than anything. He'd seen that when she'd convinced the little girl to open her bedroom door for her. Maisy wouldn't have opened it for him. She'd thought he was the monster.

And he felt a little like one now. He'd been kind of mean to Shawna. Ah, hell, he'd been unfairly mean to Shawna. He knew why Cole had broken their engagement all those years ago, but she didn't know. Now she'd lost her husband, and she had a maniac trying to kill her. But she was strong. And smart.

And a good mother. She wouldn't have done anything that would cause her daughter pain. She certainly wouldn't have killed the man her child believed was her father. He never should have suspected that she had.

He'd made a mistake. And he needed to apologize. He wanted to apologize. But when he opened his mouth to do that, he realized he'd made another mistake.

Pain radiated throughout his skull, which threatened to shatter from the force of the blow that knocked him to the ground.

Before he sank into oblivion, he reflected that if not for Teddie, he might have wished he'd died. Because Cole was certain to kill him if something happened to Shawna—to the mother of his child and the woman he'd never stopped loving.

Chapter 12

A cold sweat broke out on Cole's skin, chilling him to the bone. Where the hell was she? And where the hell was Manny?

He stared at the open door to his bedroom. The jamb wasn't broken. It wasn't as if someone had forced their way into the room. Or out of it. No windows were even open. Maybe she'd gone to stay in that little pink room with her daughter. With *their* daughter…

When would he get used to thinking of her that way? And of himself as a father? When they were able to tell Maisy—when it was safe—would she accept him as her father? Or would she always consider Emery Little to be her true dad?

Cole's stomach muscles twisted. He hated that he was jealous of a dead man. Emery had stepped up when he hadn't. Cole wasn't certain he would have if he'd known the truth. He'd had even more dangerous missions after the one that had compelled him to break his engagement to Shawna. What kind of father would he have been to the little girl when he had never been around?

He needed to be around now to make sure she was safe. He headed toward that pink bedroom. But when he tried to turn the knob, it held fast, not just locked but held tightly. When it opened, he saw why. Lars Ecklund had had his enormous hand wrapped around the knob from the other side. He and Nikki, together, guarded the little girl. No wonder she slept so peacefully, with a slight smile on her lips.

Staring at her caused that vice to tighten around his heart again. Even before he'd learned she was his, he'd begun to fall for her, just because she looked so much like her mother. But she had a part of him, too. She had his eyes.

Lars stepped out into the hall with Cole and pulled the door closed. Cole stared at that closed door, as if he could see through it. As if he could see his little girl still…

His. She was his.

"Are you okay?" Lars asked, his deep voice even deeper with concern.

"No," Cole answered honestly. He was not okay. For so many reasons.

Lars glanced back at that closed door. "She's yours." It wasn't a question. He already knew.

Apparently, everyone but him had at least suspected Maisy was a Bentler. What was the point in hiding it when Emery's killer probably already knew the truth?

Did the killer also know about the changes to the will? Cole couldn't believe that his grandfather had changed the damn thing. Had he learned nothing from what Cole had gone through after his father had changed his? What the hell had his grandfather been thinking? Was the old man losing it? No. He was as sharp and manipulative as ever. Damn him.

"Yes, she's mine," Cole said. And he wasn't going to hide it or deny it. He was just going to make damn sure she was safe. And with both Lars and Nikki protecting her, she was safe.

What about her mother?

She wasn't in the room with Maisy. He wished she'd been in there with Cooper's top two bodyguards. When they worked together, Nikki and Lars were invincible.

Before he could ask if they'd seen her, Lars reached out and squeezed his arm. "I'm sorry, man," he said. "Sorry that you just found out."

That wasn't just Shawna's fault, though. While he was furious with her, he was also angry with his grandfather. And he was a little angry with himself, as well.

When he'd heard that she'd had a baby, he should have come home. He should have insisted on a paternity test. But maybe he hadn't really wanted to know then. He'd had years left on his enlistment and had been part of the elite unit given all those special missions...

"Where are Manny and Shawna?" he asked.

Lars shrugged. "I heard them come out of the room and head down the back stairs to the kitchen."

"Kitchen?"

"Maybe she got hungry," Lars said. "It's been a long day."

And Cole couldn't remember ever seeing her eat. He nodded. "Yeah, that makes sense." But he still had that cold sweat on his skin, to the extent that goose bumps were rising beneath his clothes. He turned away from Lars and rushed toward the back stairs. His feet barely touched each step as he descended to the kitchen.

It was empty and dark but for a dim light over the sink. All the food was put away, not even a crumb left out on the marble countertops. No one had been down recently.

"Where the hell are they?" he murmured.

Then, like in Shawna's bedroom, he noticed the curtains fluttering near the patio doors in the breakfast nook. Someone had gone out on the patio. Why? It was so late. Or early? It had to be closer to dawn than to dusk now.

His hand on his holster, he stepped onto the patio. And the minute he stepped out, he noticed the body lying on the bricks. He nearly fell over it—over Manny.

He dropped to his knees beside his friend and felt for a pulse. His fingers smeared through blood trailing from Manny's head, over his throat, to pool beneath him. Despite the amount of blood, his pulse was strong and steady. The guy was tough, or he probably wouldn't have survived his childhood much less the Marine Corps and the bodyguard assignments they'd had.

"Manny," he whispered. "Hang in there." He squeezed his shoulder. And as he did, he noticed that the bodyguard's holster was empty.

Cole leaned forward to check both Manny's hands. One was beneath him, as if it had broken his fall. His right hand curled into a fist beside him; the one that would have held his weapon. If he'd still had it.

But it was gone. Like Shawna…

A rock, smeared with blood, lay near the fallen bodyguard.

His friend murmured and shifted against the patio bricks as he tried to come around, but he'd been hit hard. Too hard to regain consciousness soon. Manny wouldn't be able to help him find Shawna.

Where the hell was she? Manny wouldn't have let her get far from him. She should have been close. She would have been close, had something not happened to her. Where had the killer taken her?

Cole's heart slammed against his ribs, and his fear intensified. He never should have left her alone in that room, even with Manny outside the door. He should have personally made certain she stayed safe.

Because now, even if he found her, he might be too late to save her this time. The killer might have already ended her life.

Shawna had noticed the shadows shift across the patio as someone had approached from behind the garage. But before she could warn Manny, the shadow had swung something at him. And Manny's big body had dropped heavily to the patio.

The blow had to have been hard to make him fall like that. Would he be able to survive it?

He needed help, Shawna knew. But she couldn't get him any if she was dead. So she ran.

With the attacker between her and the house, she'd had to run away through the gardens. She could have headed toward the garage, but she'd already nearly died inside there. And she wasn't certain if the power had been turned back on. She wasn't going alone into the dark.

But it was dark beyond the house, and she stumbled and fell. An oath slipped through her lips as she hit the ground hard. The woodchips on the garden path bit into her hands and knees. She held in a cry because she could hear him.

Someone else was walking the grounds, their steps heavy but quick. He would be upon her soon. If she didn't get moving, he would probably fall right over her.

She pushed herself up, the jagged pieces of wood digging into her palms. Her heart pounding, her lungs burning for breath, she ran.

The gardens were expansive, encompassing several acres of property around the house. Maybe she could circle back around to the house. But she didn't know where the attacker was now, and if she turned back, she risked running right into him. She could hear footsteps, twigs snapping, but the sounds echoed throughout the gardens. She had no idea from where they were coming.

She was being careful to keep her steps light, and fortunately her slippers made no sound against the ground. So her footsteps weren't echoing like those of the person following her.

Had Manny's attacker gotten the bodyguard's weapon away from him? Before she'd turned and run, she'd noticed the shadow lean over Manny's body. He could have been checking for a pulse. Or he could have been grabbing the gun.

Did she have to worry about getting shot at? But no one would call a bullet in the back a suicide. Of course, the killer could get close enough to shoot her in the head.

But nobody would believe she'd killed herself. Even Manny had put aside those suspicions about her. While he obviously didn't think she was a good person, he no longer seemed to think she was a killer. He'd trusted her enough to bring her outside despite his better judgment. And she might have gotten him killed for trusting her.

Not only had she kept Cole's daughter from him, now she might have caused him to lose a friend. Maybe his best friend. In his letters, he'd written the most about Manny.

Tears stung her eyes. She blinked furiously, fighting them back. She couldn't succumb to sobbing. That would give away her location immediately. Not that she'd found the perfect spot to hide.

She kept running. Until she saw it. The gardening shed. It was big and held all the tools and equipment. When she reached the door, she found it locked. She swallowed the curse that burned her throat. Just like the sobs, she needed to hold it in.

The panic she'd been experiencing in Cole's bedroom, after he left, was nothing in comparison to the panic she felt now. Her heart was beating so furiously that it echoed inside her head, and she could barely draw a breath all for the pressure on her lungs. She was outside, like she'd wanted, and she still couldn't breathe.

She had been a fool. Such a fool. She'd given her attacker the perfect opportunity to try to kill her again. But she couldn't let him win. She couldn't let him take her away from her daughter.

Maisy...

Shawna never should have left her. She should have known then that the risk was too great that she might never return to her. She might never be able to hold her again. Would Cole hold her? Would he comfort their child? Or would he never even claim her as his?

Shawna blinked at the tears burning her eyes. She wasn't going to give in to them. She wasn't giving up. She would survive just like she had when she'd been trapped in the garage.

But she heard the woodchips crunch beneath a heavy foot. And she knew the killer was close. Too close for her to outrun. She had to hide.

She slipped around the back of the shed. A wheelbarrow had been propped up against the siding. Shawna was small enough that she could curl up in the bed of the wheelbarrow.

But she didn't move fast enough. She'd just slipped

into the hiding spot when a strong hand gripped her shoulder.

She hadn't run fast enough. Or far enough to escape.

The killer had found her.

"Noooo!" The cry of terror shattered the quiet of the room that was dark but for the almost eerie pink glow of a night-light.

Nikki closed her arms around the little girl. But Maisy thrashed in her embrace and cried, "Mommy! The monster has Mommy!"

"No," Nikki told her, her heart breaking over the child's inconsolable fear. "The monster doesn't have your mom. She's fine. She's safe." Over the little girl's head, she met Lars's gaze.

His pale blue eyes held something she rarely saw in them: fear and dread. He shook his head.

What did that mean? Of course he couldn't know for certain that Shawna was safe. She'd left the bedroom down the hall and had gone downstairs with Manny a while ago. They should have been back by now, though, especially since Cole had gone to search for them. Hopefully they were all just on the main level, in the kitchen or the library.

She mouthed the words, *Get her!*

But Lars shook his head again. He glanced down at the screen of his cell phone, at a text message lit up on it. Then he looked up at Nikki again and mouthed back, *She's gone!*

Nikki's stomach lurched as she realized that he wasn't just talking about Shawna being gone from the room down the hall. She was *gone* gone—as in nobody knowing where she was.

What about Manny? she wanted to ask. Manny wouldn't have let anyone get her—unless he'd been incapacitated. *Damn it.* What the hell had happened?

Despite their brief inaudible conversation, it was like Maisy heard them anyway. Or maybe she'd just picked up on the fear and concern that was palpable in the room. She thrashed again in Nikki's arms, struggling to escape her embrace.

"Mommy!" she cried, hysteria rising in her voice. "I want Mommy!"

The other bodyguards would find her. The Payne Protection Agency was good, so good that they had never failed an assignment before. Well, except for when they'd purposely done it because their client had been the bad guy.

But Xavier Bentler wasn't a bad guy. And neither was Shawna. Even though she'd kept Maisy's paternity secret, she wasn't a bad person. Just misguided.

Or proud and stubborn.

Nikki could identify with those traits.

"Your mommy will be here soon," she assured the little girl, and she hoped like hell she wasn't lying.

But she saw Lars flinch. He thought she was.

And so did Maisy, who cried harder. Between sobs, she said, "The monster…the monster has Mommy…"

Was it possible?

Could the monster have her?

Chapter 13

Cole ducked, dodging the fists flailing about his head and shoulders. He couldn't fight back. He could only reach out and clasp Shawna's delicate wrists. "Shh," he told her. "It's me. But…maybe you've already realized that."

She tensed, then sagged against him in relief. "Oh, thank God. Thank God."

He moved his hand to the back of her head and patted her hair. Twigs and leaves were tangled up in the silken strands. "Are you okay?"

She jerked her head up and down in a quick nod. But then she pulled away from him. "But Manny's not. He's hurt."

"I know, I know," he assured her. "I called for help for him before I started looking for you."

"Is he… Is he okay?" she asked.

Cole had no idea. The minute he'd called for help, he'd taken off in the direction of the footsteps he'd heard. He still wasn't sure if the ones he'd heard had been hers.

Or the killer's.

The killer could be out there, still, watching them.

He drew Shawna closer and reached for his holster. "We need to get back to the house." They were quite far from it, so far that he couldn't even see the light that had illuminated the patio. Nor could he see any lights burning in any of the windows. Not that anyone else was awake right now.

Except for the bodyguards and the killer.

She shivered. She was probably cold. She wore only a robe over a nightgown. Her feet were bare. Somewhere she'd lost her slippers. He'd found one near the woodchip trail. He'd been afraid that she'd lost it because someone had been carrying her. Or dragging her.

"Yes, we need to check on Manny, make sure he's all right." Now she shuddered. "I know he got hit. I saw the shadow, saw it swing something at him and Manny fell." Her voice cracked. "And I ran." She blinked, but a tear trailed down her cheek. "Like a coward."

"You were smart," he told her. "If you hadn't run away…"

The killer would have gotten ahold of her. Cole might not have found her. She would have been lost. Or dead.

He shuddered at the thought of losing her. Six

years ago, he'd given her up. He'd thought he was doing the noble thing. But he'd made a hell of a mistake. A mistake it was probably too late to fix.

Too much had happened. She'd married another man. She had passed off Cole's child as that man's. But still, Cole couldn't bring himself to hate her. He wanted to. But just like he had since the first moment he saw her, he loved her.

And with that love kicked in all of his protective instincts. So she wouldn't hurt her feet, he swung her up in his arms and carried her back toward the house. She didn't protest. She just wrapped her arm around his shoulders and clung to him.

He could feel her trembling, either from the cold or the fear she must have felt. As always, he reacted to her closeness. His pulse, which had already been racing, quickened even more. His heart beat hard and heavily, just like hers. He felt it pounding against his shoulder.

While he had one arm beneath her slight weight, holding her against him, his other hand held his weapon. He wasn't going to let anyone hurt her and not just because it was his job to protect her.

He couldn't lose her. Not that he wanted her again. It didn't matter how Cole felt about her. After what she'd done—after keeping his daughter from him— he would never be able to trust her.

And he couldn't be with someone he couldn't trust.

Just like Cole had held her and comforted her, Shawna held and comforted Maisy. But unlike Cole, who only held her for a few moments while bringing her back to the house, Shawna held her daughter until she fell asleep again.

Then she tucked her warm little body back into her bed. She wanted to say something to Nikki who sat in a chair nearby, but she didn't want to risk waking up Maisy again. The poor kid hadn't had much sleep that wasn't interrupted either with real monsters or nightmares of them.

So Shawna just nodded at Nikki before she slipped back into the hall. Cole stood outside the door. Why hadn't he come inside? Hadn't he wanted to be around his daughter?

Did he not want her to be his daughter? Did he not want to be a father?

"I'm sorry," Shawna murmured.

His eyes, the same deep blue as their daughter's, narrowed slightly. "About what?"

She expelled a shaky sigh. There were so many things. "Manny," she said. "I talked him into bringing me outside for some air."

"And nearly got you both killed," Cole finished for her.

She reached for his arm, clutching it. "Is he going to be all right?" How badly had his friend been hurt?

When Cole had carried her back to the house, Manny was no longer on the patio. But blood pooled on the bricks from his wound.

"He regained consciousness before Cooper even got to him. But the boss insisted on taking him for a CT scan."

Her stomach pitched with nausea at the thought of how seriously the other man might be hurt. As a nurse, she knew how dangerous head wounds were. The risk for subdural bleeding. For swelling on the brain.

"That's good he's getting a CT," she said. Hopefully the attending physician would have him admitted for observation. "I'm glad Cooper took him."

"He gave him a fight," another man said. The blond giant, Lars, joined them outside Maisy's room. "Dane and I had to insist."

Cole snorted. "Like either of you have the right to talk. Both you stubborn fools have fought getting treatment for concussions."

Lars's incredibly broad shoulders rose and fell in a slight shrug. "And we're both fine. Manny will be, too."

Cole nodded and released a ragged breath. "Yeah, he's got a hard head."

"The hardest," Lars agreed. It was clear they were comforting each other in that awkward, tough-love way that guys had.

The door to Maisy's room creaked open and Nikki stepped out. Before Shawna or the other bodyguards could say anything, the petite brunette assured them, "The windows are locked. Nobody can get to her before I go back inside."

Shawna relaxed slightly. She believed Nikki would keep her daughter safe.

But Cole remained tense. "We're short Cooper and Manny until they get back," he said. "We need to stick extra close to Shawna and my…" he drew in a breath, as if bracing himself, before continuing "…daughter."

Shawna's heart flipped. He'd claimed her. If something happened to Shawna, Maisy would not be alone. She'd have her father. Her family.

But Cole believed one of them was a killer.

"And we need to be aware that if the killer wasn't armed before, he definitely has a gun now," Cole warned the other bodyguards.

Lars flinched. "He got Manny's weapon off him?"

Shawna doubted Manny had had much choice. He'd clearly been knocked out cold before he ever hit the patio.

Cole nodded. Nikki cursed.

"Does it matter?" Shawna asked as hysteria began to well up in her fiercely pounding heart. She had never been so afraid—not even when she'd been a little girl alone in the world after her parents had died. "Is Manny's gun any more lethal than a bomb or carbon monoxide or a rope?"

All the bodyguards stared at her as if she was crazy. But then she didn't know the dangers they knew. She only knew the dangers she'd faced. She wasn't one of them. This wasn't the life she had chosen. She wanted no part of it—of any of it. She'd mistakenly thought she could once handle it when Cole had left for boot camp. But when he'd been deployed...

She had lived in fear that something would happen to him. Maybe he'd been right to break up with her then. Maybe she wouldn't have been able to handle being the wife of a man who constantly put himself in danger.

"A gun is faster," Cole replied. "And once a bullet is fired, it's hard to stop it from hitting its target."

So the killer would be able to kill her faster and easier now that he had Manny's gun. Her legs began to tremble, threatening to fold beneath her.

"Target," she repeated Cole's word. Then she clarified. "Me. I'm the target."

"We'll protect you," Nikki assured her.

But this time Cole made no such promise to her. He only stared at her. And she had no idea what he was thinking or feeling.

Was he so angry with her over keeping Maisy from him that he didn't care anymore if she lived or died? She could hardly blame him. It hadn't happened yet, but she was furious at the thought of her attacker trying to take her away from her daughter, like she had kept Cole away.

But if he'd known, would he have come back to her? Not that it mattered. She wouldn't have wanted him back like that—just because of their child. She'd wanted him back because he loved her—like she had always loved him. And always would…until the day she died. Unfortunately that day might not be far off. The killer was determined to get to her.

"Why?" she asked them. "Why am I a target?" She had no money. No enemies but for Cole. Why was someone trying to kill her?

Lars and Nikki shook their heads. They had no answers for her. But Cole looked away. He already suspected that someone in his family was responsible. Did he know why one of them would want her dead?

The killer stared at the gun held in a gloved hand. The Glock was easy enough to use. Slide off the safety and squeeze the trigger. When Shawna had fallen on the garden path, it would have been easy to shoot her.

But the gunshot would have drawn the attention of the other bodyguards—would have brought help right away. Not that it had taken Cole long to rush to her rescue.

No. The new plan—the one that had replaced the brilliant murder-suicide plan—was to kill Cole first. But Shawna going outside, with just the one bodyguard for protection, had just presented too good an opportunity to pass up. Once the bodyguard had been incapacitated, she would have been so easy to kill.

But for Cole's damn untimely arrival.

Shooting Cole then would have been as risky as shooting her. The sound of the gunshot would have brought all the bodyguards rushing in to help just the same.

Cole's death had to be planned out precisely. It had to allow enough time for the killer to escape without detection from the murder scene.

But Cole was going to die. Soon.

Chapter 14

Cole could see that Shawna wanted promises from him. She was still standing outside her daughter's bedroom door. Lars and Nikki were also in the hall with them.

Shawna stared up at him, quietly beseeching him. He fully intended to do everything within his power to keep her alive, even if he had to take the bullet for her. And that was what he didn't want to tell her.

He didn't want to point out the dangers of his job. He already had his grandfather and Cooper conspiring to remove him from this assignment. But there was no way in hell he was leaving this house now, not with Shawna and their daughter in danger.

Cooper was gone now, though. So Cole stepped into his place as lead. "Dane's guarding the outside door," he said. "Lars, you take this hall, and Nikki, stay in Maisy's room. I'll bring Shawna back to mine."

He expected her to resist, but she said nothing, just let him lead her back into the room she'd left earlier with Manny. She shivered as he closed the door behind them. No windows were open in this room, but she might have still been cold from running around outside in the gardens.

"Are you okay?" he asked. She was probably in shock.

She gave him a faint nod, as if she wasn't quite certain herself.

He looked closer. In addition to the bruising on her throat from the earlier attempt on her life, he noticed the cuts on her knees and hands. "You're hurt," he said.

She turned over her hands and glanced down at her dirty, bloodied palms. "I fell."

He suppressed a shudder at how close the killer must have come to catching her. Whoever the hell it was, he'd gotten too close—too many times. Despite himself, Cole offered the promise she'd sought earlier. "I will protect you," he vowed.

She released a shaky little breath of relief but then she stared up at him and asked, "Are you sure you want to?"

"It's my job," he reminded her. But she was a hell of a lot more than that to him. She was everything. She had always been...

Everything.

"I'm sorry," she said.

"You already apologized for getting Manny to take

you outside," he reminded her. But he didn't actually think that was what she was apologizing for this time. Would she, though? Would she apologize for keeping Maisy from him?

And would he accept if she did? Could he forgive her? Even while he still cared about her—hell, still loved her—he was furious with her. But she wasn't the only one he was angry with.

"I'm sorry your grandfather got you caught up in all this," she said.

"You shouldn't apologize for my grandfather," he told her. Not when she was probably in danger because of the wily old codger. "And we didn't have to accept this assignment."

"You said Cooper gave you no choice," she reminded him.

He sighed and admitted, "I could have fought him harder." Or he could have told Cooper the truth—that he wasn't over her, that he would never get over her. But he suspected his very intuitive friend already knew that.

"Why didn't you?" she asked.

He stepped closer. "I didn't and I don't want you to be in any danger, Shawna." And that was why he had to be careful. He had to make sure no one knew how he felt about her yet.

Not even her.

"You haven't changed your mind since you found out about Maisy?" she asked. Her voice cracked and her eyes glistened with unshed tears. "You don't hate me."

"I want to," he admitted.

"I would understand if you did," she told him.

Maybe that was why she'd kept their child a secret—
because she'd wanted him to hate her like she'd hated
him. She must have, to keep Maisy from him. And that
was his fault. For the things he'd said when he'd broken
their engagement. For the way he'd acted, as if she'd
meant nothing to him.

He stepped closer and touched her hands. They
were smeared with dirt and blood. Even then, he
wanted them on him, wanted her to touch him like
he wanted to touch her.

"You should clean up." He pointed her toward the
attached bathroom.

He needed a moment alone to gather his thoughts
and his control. Right now his body ached with
need for hers. He wanted her. Despite everything,
he wanted her.

Shawna wanted Cole. She wanted him to hold her.
To forgive her.

Most of all, she wanted him to love her. But had
he ever? How could he have broken their engagement
and her heart like he had?

She flinched as she turned off the shower faucet.
Despite washing them, her hands still stung with the
little cuts and scrapes from the woodchips. Her knees
had fared a little better. But she'd needed to wash her
feet, too, since she had lost her slippers somewhere
along the garden trail.

So she'd just climbed into the shower, letting the
spray wash over her naked body. She'd wanted Cole's

hands on her, moving over her bare skin, heating up her flesh to chase away the chill. And the fear.

She was so afraid. Afraid of losing her life. And afraid of losing her heart.

Why didn't he hate her? For all the years she'd kept Maisy from him, he had the right. If the situation had been reversed, she would have hated him. Did he not care enough about her? Or Maisy?

Knuckles brushed across the wood of the bathroom door and a deep voice called out, "Are you all right?"

And she knew that he cared—at least a little bit— about her still.

She stepped out of the shower and reached for a towel. As she did, she opened her mouth to answer him. But he opened the door before she had the chance.

His gaze swept over her naked body. Just that warmed her, had her blood pumping fast and hot through her veins.

She wanted him. And she could see, with the passion darkening his eyes, that he wanted her, as well. He reached for her. But instead of jerking her into his arms, pulling her closer, he reached for the towel. He ran the soft fabric over her skin, drying her. He lifted the towel to her hair and squeezed the water from her long tresses.

She thought fleetingly of how she bathed and dried Maisy. But this was nothing like that. This was not maternal, although it was gentle. It was hot as hell, like the look in his eyes.

He slid the towel from her hair to her waist, then

he used it to propel her toward him. "Are you all right?" he asked again, but this time his voice was gruff with emotion.

She shook her head. "No."

He touched her throat and then ran his fingertips along her bare arms to her hands. "What hurts?"

She caught her hand in his and pulled it toward her breast, toward her heart that pounded madly with passion for him. "This hurts…" she murmured.

His hand closed over her breast, and her nipple tightened and pushed against his palm. Her breath caught at the exquisite sensation. It had been so long since she'd been touched like this.

"Cole…"

He shook his head, as if trying to deny that he wanted her, too. But she could feel the tension in him, could see his pulse beating erratically in his throat.

He wanted her just as much as she wanted him. Maybe more—he swung her up in his arms and carried her toward the bed. Like before, he followed her down as he lowered her to the mattress.

But she didn't let him hold himself away from her. She clutched him close and tore at his clothes, trying to pull up his shirt. It caught on the holster.

He reached for his gun.

She tensed beneath him, fearful that he'd heard something. That the killer was back. That he would give her no rest.

Or no pleasure.

But Cole removed the gun and the holster, laying them on the small table beside the bed. He dragged his shirt over his head, muscles rippling in his arms and chest. He was broader than he'd been six years ago, more muscular. And along with the muscles, there were a few scars—a jagged little ridge on one shoulder and another along his ribs.

She touched them tentatively. "What happened?"

He shook his head. And she didn't know if he didn't want to talk about it or if he couldn't. What had he endured during all those missions with the Marine Corps and as a bodyguard?

She leaned forward and pressed her lips to the scar on his shoulder. Then she wriggled beneath him until she was able to press her lips to the scar along his ribs.

His breath shuddered out in a ragged sigh. And her name. "Shawna…"

Then he was the one to slip down the bed, down her body, pressing his lips to every inch of her skin. She shivered even while heat coursed through her. He kissed her shoulders and her arms and her breasts. His mouth moved over the mound before his lips closed around a nipple and gently tugged.

She cried out at the exquisite pleasure and tension wound tightly inside her. She needed him so badly and reached for his belt, unclasped it and pulled down his zipper.

His breath hissed out between his teeth. She stroked her fingers over his erection, which strained against his boxer briefs. Then she pushed down the material, and it was like he stopped breathing entirely as she stroked her fingers down the engorged length of him.

"Shawna…" He groaned her name. Then he pulled back and stood up.

Did he not want her touching him? Had he changed his mind about making love with her?

He didn't walk away. Instead he kicked off his shoes and pushed down his pants and boxers. Then he stood gloriously naked before her.

But he was too far away. She held out her hands, silently pleading with him to come back to bed. Back to her...

She knew that would never happen. Six years had passed, and he had never once contacted her in all that time. If not for Xavier manipulating him, he wouldn't have come back now. Remembering that should have brought her to her senses, should have made her stop. But she wanted him too much to deny that desire now that need.

He rooted around in his pocket before pulling out a condom packet. He tore it open and rolled it on his erection.

Seeing him in real life again, instead of just in her dreams, she tensed and wondered how they had ever fit together. He was so big. When they'd made love before, he would take his time with her, make sure she was ready. But they weren't making love now. They weren't in love. At least he wasn't in love with her.

Would he just take her?

Instead of fear, excitement coursed through her. It had been so long, she didn't care. She was ready for him.

But like all those times before, he made sure. When he joined her back on the bed, he kissed her tenderly and then with more heat. His tongue slid inside her mouth, and his fingers slid inside her body, teasing her, making her crazy. Making her ready.

She rose up from the mattress with a cry of frustration. She wanted him.

But he was moving away again, moving down her body. He replaced his fingers with his lips and his tongue. And the tension inside her shattered as an orgasm came over her. Then he was there, easing his erection inside her, and she arched and shifted until she could take him deep. Despite the six years that had passed, they moved together in perfect rhythm, a dance they'd danced several times.

It had been years since they'd danced together like this. Six long years since Shawna had been with him, since she'd been with anyone.

She had only ever been with Cole. He was the only man she'd ever wanted, that she had ever loved. And she loved him still. He'd broken her heart, but it still belonged to him. She poured that love into her kisses, into her touches...into her movements.

The tension wound tightly inside her again. His deep strokes set her off again, another orgasm shuddering through her body with an intensity she'd never known. Maybe it was just because it had been so long.

Or maybe it was just because it was Cole. The feelings she had for him were even deeper now.

He thrust again and then he called out as he came. For a few short seconds, he leaned his forehead against hers and stared into her eyes. She wasn't certain what he was looking for.

Love?

Regret?

Guilt?

She felt all of those things for him. Most of all, she loved him. And she wanted to tell him. But was that fair? Sure, he would probably never return her feelings. He would never be able to forgive her for not telling him about Maisy. Hell, she would never forgive herself for that.

Maybe it was better that he hate her anyway. The killer after her was determined, so determined that he was probably destined to succeed. It would be easier for Cole if he didn't know how she felt about him, that she loved him, that she'd never stopped loving him.

She tensed as a sudden thought occurred to her. Was that what he had been doing for her six years ago? Instead of breaking her heart, had he been trying to protect it, like he'd always tried to protect her?

He'd told her, had warned her, that his missions kept getting more and more dangerous. Had he thought he wouldn't make it back from that one? Was that why he'd broken up with her?

He had made it back, though.

But she'd already been married to another man. Regret slammed through her, stopping her heart for a millisecond. That could have been why he acted so betrayed. Maybe he had only been trying to protect her, and he thought she'd moved on, that she'd never really cared.

She wanted to tell him the truth, wanted to tell her that she never had a real relationship with Emery. But she couldn't do that to him—not now. Not when she was in so much danger. No. It was better for him to hate her. Still.

It was better that he not know that she loved him. That she had always loved him. She closed her eyes, so that he wouldn't see it, wouldn't see the love.

When she opened her eyes again, even though only seconds had passed, he was gone. Not far; she could hear him in the attached bathroom. But realistically, he'd been gone for six years, and he still wasn't back. Despite them making love, he was still gone from her.

When he walked back into the bedroom, she pretended she was sleeping. He didn't join her anyway. She could hear the floor creaking as he paced before the windows, protecting her just as he'd promised he would. He didn't crawl into bed and take her into his arms. He didn't hold her like he used to after they made love.

And she knew it didn't matter what she told him; he didn't return her feelings. She'd killed whatever love he'd felt for her when she'd married another man. And even if she lived, she wasn't certain he would ever forgive her or come to love her again. So it was good that she hadn't told him the truth.

She only hoped she wouldn't wind up carrying the secret of her love to her grave.

Cooper breathed a sigh of relief as he squinted against the sun shining brightly through the blinds in Xavier's den. It was morning, edging toward noon actually.

And that was good.

The person they'd been hired to protect and all of Cooper's team had survived the night. He glanced over at Manny who looked a little worse for wear, but the concussion was slight. It was hardly affecting him other than what was probably a hell of a headache. But Manny was too proud to admit he was in any pain.

Unfortunately so was Cole. If he'd admitted how much this assignment would affect him, Cooper would have never taken it. But then if something had happened to Shawna—and without their protection, it most certainly would have—Cole would have been in even more pain, emotionally.

Of course, Cooper suspected he was also in danger physically. He looked over the desk at the old man sitting behind it. Xavier had made a horrible mess of this assignment and of his grandson's life. Regret hung heavy on him, though, making his shoulders stoop with the burden of it. He already knew what Cooper thought of his manipulation. Now Cooper wished he hadn't said anything at all.

It didn't matter, though. Nothing mattered but finding the killer and stopping him. "So it has to be someone in this house," Cooper surmised. "Someone in your family."

The old man nodded. "And they all live here."

Cole didn't. But he was still in the house. He'd ignored Cooper's orders to return to River City the night before, but he had to see that he couldn't stay here. He couldn't remain on this assignment. If the killer learned how Xavier had changed his will, Cole would be in even more danger than Shawna was.

And he couldn't protect her and their daughter if he was dead.

A chill chased over Cooper's skin, making him

shudder. It was his damn sixth sense again. He'd started getting what his mom had, the ability to just *know* when something bad was about to happen. He had that feeling now more intensely than he'd ever felt it before.

Something bad—something *very* bad—was about to happen.

"We need to get Cole out of here," Cooper said. But he wasn't talking to Xavier. He was talking to Manny. He had a feeling they might have to physically remove Cole in order to get him to leave.

"He's gone." It was Lars, standing in the open door to the den. "He left his room a while ago."

"Where the hell did he go?" Cooper asked.

Lars shrugged. "I don't know. He took off down the back stairs, so I figured he was going to the kitchen." The blond giant tensed, as if he had the same premonition as Cooper. Or maybe he just picked up on Cooper's concern. "But he wasn't there."

"We need to find him!" Cooper said.

Before it was too late—if it wasn't already.

Chapter 15

The sun shone down on Cole, warming his skin on the outside. But he was still cold inside. At least he wanted to be cold. He wanted to be numb. Instead he felt too much.

Shawna made him feel too much. Last night. In the bathroom and the bedroom…

He'd felt so much desire, so much passion. But then after she'd fallen asleep, he'd felt something even more. All the love he'd always had for her surged through his heart again, and he'd been overwhelmed.

And scared.

He understood now why she'd had the urgent need to get some air the night before. But Cole had forced himself to wait until morning before he'd stepped out into the hall. Lars and Dane had just been switching posts. So she had a fresh guard in Dane, or as fresh as any of them could be after a sleepless night. But they'd all endured sleepless nights before, a lot of them in far more dangerous places than his grandfather's estate.

"You get any rest?" Lars had asked him.

Cole had just shaken his head and hurried down the back stairs before either friend could ask him more questions. And before Maisy could wake up.

He wanted to see her, but he wasn't sure he could trust himself around her. She was bound to notice how he would look at her—with wonder, with awe, with love.

He didn't know her, but he loved her. She was part of him. But that wasn't why he loved her. He loved her because she was part of Shawna. Even if she hadn't been his, he would have come to love her just because of that.

Knowing she was his made him want to claim her to the world but most especially to her. He wanted her to know that she hadn't lost her daddy, at least not her only one. He wanted her to know that he was her daddy, too. That he would do his best to fill the hole Emery Little's death had left in her young life.

But would she want him? Would she want another father at all, let alone *him*?

He didn't know what to do, how to act. His father had loved Cole, but he'd never been around that much, between his businesses and his other activities. Cole hadn't even known about Natalie. Why had his father never told him about his true love and how he'd lost her? Had he felt responsible for her death? Had he felt guilty?

There were things like that in Cole's past that he would never be able to tell Maisy. Even when she was older, he wouldn't tell her about his missions, about the dangers he'd faced. The dangers that, as a body-guard, he continued to face.

Was it fair for him to tell Maisy he was her father only to leave her life just as Emery had? Not that Cole had any intention of dying now. He'd survived all sorts of dangerous missions. Surely, he could sur-vive his bodyguard assignments, as well.

Except for maybe this one.

This one—thanks to his grandfather—was his most dangerous yet. So maybe he should wait to tell Maisy that he was her father. Maybe he should wait until they had identified and apprehended the killer.

Who could it be? His family was ruthless and greedy. But which one of them was ruthless and greedy enough to kill? Or maybe it wasn't just one. Maybe it was a couple of them acting together. His male cous-ins? Or the twins? They were female, but they were tall and strong. One of them could have knocked out Astin and Manny and wrapped that noose around Shawna's throat. Or perhaps it was his uncles, who'd grown tired of waiting for their father to die.

He tensed as he realized that in order for anyone to inherit anything, his grandfather had to die. Of course he was already eighty-six and not in the greatest of health since his heart attack. But…

Was that what this was about? The only reason someone would try to eliminate other heirs would be because they were pretty damn certain they were about to inherit. Maybe they thought Xavier would have another heart attack. It was damn well a possibility if something happened to Shawna. Either he would die of grief or because there would be no one to stop him indulging all his vices.

The change to Grandfather's will hadn't put just her in danger. It put Cole in danger, as well.

Just then, he noticed a flash.

The sunlight was glinting off something metallic. No sooner had he realized that the metallic thing was a gun than the shot rang out.

And he had no doubt the bullet was headed right toward him.

Maisy screamed and jerked away from Shawna, who'd been pulling a dress over the little girl's head. Shawna held in her own cry of alarm. She'd heard it, too, and had felt the windows rattle from the sharp noise.

Nikki jumped out of the chair where she'd been slumped in exhaustion, close to the bed. Suddenly very awake and alert, her hand automatically reached for her weapon.

"Was that a bomb, Mommy?" Maisy asked, her little body trembling with fear. "Was that another bomb?"

Shawna shook her head. "No. That wasn't a bomb."

"What was it?"

"I—I don't know…" But she knew, as she watched Nikki draw her weapon from her holster, that it had been a gunshot. Another shot rang out and another.

Maisy screamed again.

Fear coursed through Shawna. But she wasn't

being fired at. While the shots were close enough to rattle the windows, the bullets hadn't shattered the glass. The gunshots weren't being fired into the house. The shots came from outside the house, but close by.

"Where—where's Cole?" she asked Nikki in a whisper. When she'd awakened, she hadn't seen him. Had he gone to another room or had he left the estate entirely?

"He went downstairs just a little while ago," Nikki murmured as she peered through the window.

And Shawna knew those shots had been fired at Cole.

"Is Cole okay, Mommy?" Maisy asked fearfully, all of her concern for a man she'd just met. She didn't even know that he was her father.

At least Shawna didn't think she knew. It was hard to say what the intuitive little girl had picked up on. She often eavesdropped on adult conversations and might have heard one of the Bentlers speculating about her paternity. Did she know Cole was her daddy? Is that why she was so worried that he was in danger?

Shawna pulled her daughter into her arms to comfort her. But if Cole had been shot, she would need comforting, too. She needed Cole. She'd needed him when she'd lost her parents. She didn't know how she would have survived without his friendship and support. She'd needed him six years ago, too, when he'd broken up with her. She'd needed him to help raise their daughter. But he hadn't been around, and she'd managed.

But that had been different because she'd known that he was still alive and well.

Even as angry as she'd been with him, she had never wished him any harm. She'd prayed during every one of his deployments that he would survive his mission. She hadn't realized then that the most danger he might face would be protecting her.

He had to be okay.

Xavier heard the gunshot. It was close to the house, close to his den. He jumped up from his chair, but his head swam and he had to plant his palms on his desk to steady himself.

It was hell getting old. Since his damn heart attack, he couldn't stand up quickly without getting light-headed. Or maybe it was because he'd hardly slept last night for all the thoughts and fears racing through his mind. What had he done?

Cole didn't give a damn about the money. He didn't want it. Neither would Shawna. Xavier had been crazy to change his will. It hadn't brought Cole and Shawna back together like he'd planned. All it had accomplished was to put them in danger. Poor Emery Little had died. And Shawna and Astin had nearly died the day before.

More gunshots rang out. Who the hell was firing and at whom? Had a bullet struck someone?

He needed to go check. He needed to make sure nobody was hurt. But he had a bad feeling that someone was and he knew who. And it wasn't Shawna. After last night, no Payne Protection bodyguard would have allowed Shawna to step outside the house again.

So that left Cole.

Had the others found him? They'd rushed out of

the den to search for him just minutes before that first gunshot rang out. It was almost as if Cooper Payne had somehow known Cole was in danger. But of course he had, he'd already warned Xavier that his manipulations had put his grandson in danger.

Had Cole survived all those damn dangerous missions only to get killed at home? Xavier had been a fool to bring him back here—to put his life at risk.

That bad feeling spread to Xavier's chest and radiated down his arm. And then it wasn't just bad. It was painful.

Oh, damn...

He was having another heart attack. And he'd been warned that he was too old, his heart too damaged, to handle another one.

But hell, maybe that was karma after all the trouble he'd caused, and not just now for Cole and Shawna. He'd caused a hell of a lot of trouble in his eighty-six years. His troublemaking had cost him marriages, friendships, a business partner and the love of his life. Yeah, this was probably karma.

He clutched at his chest as if he could somehow hold his heart together. But if Cole had been shot, there would be no fixing it. And if Cole was dead, Xavier didn't care about himself.

He didn't call out, not that he had much time before his legs folded beneath him and he dropped to the floor.

Chapter 16

Pain radiated from Cole's shoulder. He rolled it and winced as the bruised muscle rippled beneath his skin.

"Were you hit?" Manny asked anxiously.

Cole shook his head. "I'm fine. I just hit my shoulder when I dove out of the way." He studied the hole in the brick wall of the house. He'd been standing close to where the first bullet had burrowed into the mortar between the bricks. Other bullets had chipped into the wall, but those hadn't gotten as close. He wasn't certain if the shooter was a bad marksman or if he'd chickened out.

Cole had drawn his gun and returned fire in the direction he'd seen the glint of metal. But he hadn't been able to see the shooter.

"Did I hit him?" he asked. It would have been a damn lucky blind shot.

When Manny and Cooper had rushed out of the house, Cole had pointed them toward the gardens. The shooter must have stood behind the arbor, concealed in the shadows of the thick vines.

Manny shook his head, then flinched as if moving it hurt him. Cole didn't need to know the results of the CT scan to know that his friend had a concussion. He'd seen the blood on the patio the night before. It had stained the bricks near where Cole had dropped to avoid getting shot.

"I don't think so," Manny said. "We didn't see any blood spatter."

"Just these shells," Cooper said, and he opened his hand to show the spent shells lying against his palm.

"From my gun," Manny murmured with frustration and remorse. "I'm sure they're from mine."

"It doesn't matter where they're from," Cooper assured him, trying to ease Manny's guilt. "It matters who fired them. We need to find the shooter."

But he was gone. For now. Cole knew that he would be back, though. The killer kept coming back to try again, for Shawna and for him. And once he learned that Maisy was a Bentler, he would probably try for her, as well.

Cole couldn't risk it.

He couldn't risk Shawna and Maisy getting hurt. He couldn't risk his family hurting his…family. Shawna and Maisy were his family now.

And he had to do whatever was necessary to protect them.

* * *

Shawna felt trapped in her fear. Nikki wouldn't let her leave the room to check on Cole, and she'd had to wait. Finally there was a knock at Maisy's bedroom door, and his deep voice called out, "It's me."

The minute Nikki holstered her gun and opened the door, Shawna threw her arms around Cole and pressed her body against his. Her face buried in his chest, she was barely aware of Nikki stepping out of the room and closing the door behind her. "Thank God you're all right!"

Nikki had told her that he was; she'd read Shawna the text she'd received from Lars saying that Cole was okay. But Shawna hadn't really accepted it until now. Until she saw him. Felt him.

But something propelled Shawna to step back. And yet, it wasn't Cole pushing her away; a little body burrowed between them, and Maisy wound her arms around Cole's legs. He lifted her up, and the little girl clasped his neck and laid her head on his shoulder.

Shawna's heart swelled with love for both of them. Then guilt constricted it. She had been so wrong to keep the truth from them.

"I'm so glad you didn't get blowed up," Maisy said.

"There was no bomb," Cole told her.

"But I heard a 'splosion."

Over Maisy's head, Cole met Shawna's gaze. She implored him to be careful with what he revealed. But Cole shook his head. He obviously had no intention of lying, or even of withholding the truth. Which probably meant he intended to tell Maisy the truth about everything. Even that he was father.

Shawna drew in a deep breath, bracing herself for whatever he might say and for however Maisy might react.

"That noise you heard," Cole said, "was a gun going off." But before Maisy could do more than gasp, he assured her, "Nobody got hurt, though."

Maisy uttered a sigh of relief, but instead of loosening her arms around Cole's neck, she tightened them. "I was scared," she said. "Especially when Mommy asked Nikki where you were."

Heat rushed to Shawna's face. Despite trying to reassure her daughter, she'd frightened her more—because she'd revealed her own fear.

"I'm fine," he assured the little girl. He gently cupped the back of her head in his palm the way he used to do Shawna. But then he'd bring Shawna's face to his and kiss her, like he'd kissed her last night. He'd kissed her so many times over the years. But still it hadn't been enough. It would never be enough for Shawna.

"I'm glad you're okay," Maisy said. She lifted her head from his shoulder and stared into his face, into his eyes. And then, out of the blue, she asked, "Are you my daddy?"

Shawna sucked in a breath. Not that she should have been surprised. She knew her little girl was intuitive, too much so sometimes. "Why—why would you ask that?" she stammered.

Maisy's face flushed, and she lowered her gaze. She knew she wasn't supposed to be eavesdropping so she reluctantly admitted, "I hear Grampa's family talking in the house." She looked up again, but at Cole. "I heard some of your friends talking."

Cole's face flushed. "Did Nikki say anything to you?"

"She thought I was sleeping," Maisy said. "She was talking to Lars."

"Of course," Cole murmured.

"You shouldn't eavesdrop," Shawna admonished the little girl.

"It's how I find out things," Maisy said. "Important things."

"But not everything you hear is the truth," Shawna cautioned her. "It might just be people speculating."

"Speck-u-whating?" Maisy repeated.

"Just gossiping," Shawna said. "Guessing. They don't know the truth."

Maisy turned toward her. She and Cole both stared at Shawna, their identical pairs of blue eyes narrowed. Cole waited for a long moment, as if he was waiting for her to say it first.

But then he must have concluded that she couldn't be trusted to tell the truth. "This time, Maisy, the speculation wasn't gossip. It was true. It is true."

The little girl turned back to him and lifted her hand to his face. She stared deeply into his eyes, maybe in recognition that they were nearly the same, because she said with absolute certainty, "You are my daddy."

His jaw clenched so tightly a muscle twitched in his cheek, and he just nodded.

Maisy turned back to Shawna, and her little brow furrowed with confusion. "Did you know?"

Shawna gasped again. Her little girl never failed to surprise her. "I— Yes, I knew. But Cole didn't know until yesterday. He was gone a long time."

"And I had a daddy," Maisy said.

Cole flinched.

"But that daddy's dead now," Maisy said. She patted Cole's cheek again. "I don't want you to die, too."

He shook his head. "I don't want to die either. And I want to keep you and your mommy safe, too. That's why you need to pack up your favorite clothes and toys."

"Where are we going?" Maisy asked.

Was he taking their daughter away just as Shawna had feared? Was this his revenge on her for not letting him know she'd had his child?

She would fight him, just as desperately as she'd fought to get out of that garage and away from the intruder.

"I'm going to take you someplace safe," Cole said.

Maisy asked the question burning in Shawna's mind: "What about Mommy?"

"I'm going to take you and your mommy someplace safe," Cole assured her.

Shawna shook her head, but she waited until Cole set their daughter down. While Maisy rushed over to her closet to collect her favorite toys, Shawna grasped Cole's arm and tugged him toward the door. "I want to talk to you," she murmured.

He nodded and opened the door. As they stepped out, Nikki stepped back inside to protect Maisy. Before closing the door between them, the female bodyguard told Cole, "I'm glad you're all right."

Shawna suspected those shots had come closer to hitting Cole than he'd admitted.

The minute Nikki closed the door and they were

alone, Shawna asked, "What the hell do you think you're doing?"

"I'm protecting you and our daughter," he replied. "I'm getting you out of this house."

"I can't leave," Shawna told him.

"Why the hell not?" he asked. "Someone in this house killed your husband and has tried and nearly succeeded at killing you. And now they're trying for me, too, and damn near succeeded again."

Her heart contracted with fear. Sure, she'd love to run off somewhere with him and their daughter and hide from the danger. But she shook her head. "I can't leave here because I can't leave your grandfather."

Cole clasped his hand around her wrist and tugged her toward the stairs. "Let's talk to him," he said. "I'm sure I can make him fire you."

She was sure he could, too. Xavier cared about her and he loved Maisy. He would fire her for certain if he thought it would protect her. But then who would protect him?

"He needs me," Shawna said.

Cole snorted. "He's not an invalid. He's tough as hell."

"He's an old man with a bad heart," Shawna said. "And he doesn't take care of himself. He needs me."

And she'd neglected him. Since the explosion, she hadn't been watching over him like she should. She hadn't been making certain that he took his meds and stayed away from the cigars and scotch.

As they neared the den, she quickened her step. She felt so guilty for having been remiss in her duties. Of course she was well aware that hadn't been Xavier's only motive for hiring her. She'd thought then that he'd only wanted to spend more time with Maisy, especially after his heart attack when he'd realized how precious life was. She should have realized he was up to something else, like probably getting her back together with Cole.

Of course, Emery had still been alive when Xavier had hired her. But then, Xavier had always known that theirs wasn't a real marriage.

The door stood ajar, like someone had left the den in a hurry. She pushed it open and peered inside anyway. But there was no one inside. Of course the gunshots would have drawn him out of the den.

"Was he outside with you?" she asked.

Cole shook his head and pushed the door farther. "No, he didn't come out on the patio at all."

That was weird. Xavier wasn't the type to avoid danger. He was the type to put himself in danger because of others.

She stepped into the room. And then she saw him, lying on the floor behind his desk. He was face down in a pool of something foamy looking.

"Oh, my God," she murmured in horror.

She froze for just a moment. Fear filled her that she was too late, that he was already gone. Then she dropped to her knees beside him and focused on saving him. If she could...

If she wasn't already too late...

She was too late. She had to be too late. The killer stood with the others, outside the den, watching as Shawna worked on Xavier.

Somebody murmured that the gunshots must have

brought on a heart attack. If that were true, Xavier had been down a long time. Those shots had been fired a while ago.

How had they missed? How had every damn bullet missed hitting Cole?

It must have been the gun. The sight had to be off. Or maybe it had been fired from too far away. Because Cole should have been dead, instead of standing anxiously over Shawna as she worked on his grandfather.

She'd pulled out a black bag, like she was a doctor rather than an old man's nurse and companion. But Xavier had hired her away from the ER, so she must have experience and training in trauma. In saving lives…

First, she'd pushed a device into his mouth and suctioned out something white and foamy. When she could get no more, she put an oxygen mask over his face. But the old man's eyes—those Bentler-blue eyes—remained closed. Despite all her efforts, he didn't regain consciousness. He could not regain consciousness.

In the distance, sirens wailed as an ambulance approached. But they would be too late, as well.

Wasn't the old man dead already? Xavier was old and weak. He couldn't survive another heart attack. That was what his doctor had told all of them. He would have already had another, if Shawna hadn't been here taking care of him. She was all that had stood between him and another heart attack. That was why she had needed to die.

But now it looked like Xavier would instead.

So maybe Shawna could live. But Cole—Cole still had to die—even sooner now.

Chapter 17

Cole closed his eyes. For the first time in years, he felt tears burning his eyes. If he let himself, he could have cried. He wanted to cry. But instinct had him fighting back those tears. Really there was no reason for them. He blinked his eyes open and focused on the doctor standing over his grandfather. "You're sure?"

He couldn't believe it.

"It wasn't a heart attack," the doctor assured him.

"Then what the hell was it?" Cole asked. Fear still gripped him. He couldn't forget how he and Shawna had found the old man, lying face down in his own vomit. He'd been certain he was dead. And even though the man was old, Cole wasn't ready to lose his grandfather.

"It was some kind of other episode," the doctor replied, as if he was choosing his words carefully.

"Episode?" Shawna asked. She stood beside the hospital bed, next to Cole. "We found him unconscious."

And she'd sprung into nurse mode, suctioning the vomit from his mouth so he didn't aspirate. Then she'd given him oxygen. While Xavier hadn't regained consciousness yet, Shawna had probably saved his life.

Cole had seen up close and personal the woman Shawna had become. He'd known the girl for years, what seemed like all of his life. But now he was getting to know the woman—the nurse, the mother. She was nothing like the damsel in distress he'd accused her of being. Even then, he'd known she wasn't weak and helpless. But he'd had no idea exactly how strong she was, how capable of taking care of not just herself but others, as well.

"He had vomited," Shawna was saying.

"And that might have been what saved his life," the doctor said.

Shawna nodded as if she'd gotten confirmation of some question she hadn't asked yet. "The blood you've taken—have you ordered tox screening on it?"

"Yes," the doctor replied. "And I'll notify the authorities as soon as the results are back."

Realization dawned on Cole. He waited until the doctor left before he turned to Shawna. "You think someone poisoned him?"

"I don't know for sure," she said. "It's been a long few days for him. He's been drinking too much alcohol, smoking too many cigars." Regret passed through her eyes. "That's my fault."

"You haven't been pouring the scotch or lighting his cigars," Cole told her.

"And I haven't been stopping him the past few days," she said, clearly beating herself up, "like I should have been."

"You were a little busy," Cole reminded her. "Nearly getting blown up and nearly getting suffocated in a garage and getting…" Emotion choked him as he thought of everything she had recently endured. Despite all that, she'd been taking care of their daughter and his grandfather, as well.

Cole could imagine just how much of a caregiver she was when she wasn't preoccupied with planning a memorial for her dead husband and trying to stay alive herself. She had to be unstoppable.

Was that why someone was trying to kill her? Because she stood between his grandfather and whoever was trying to kill him? The thought had occurred to him once already—just before he'd gotten shot—that someone had gotten sick of waiting for the old man to die.

But Shawna had been keeping Xavier alive. Maybe someone had wanted to get her out of the way. Maybe they didn't even know that Grandfather had changed his will.

But if they were made aware…

"I need to call Cooper," he said. They needed reinforcements. His grandfather needed guards at the hospital to make sure he wasn't in danger. If the toxicology report came back that he'd been poisoned, then

Xavier was the one somebody really wanted dead. And they would undoubtedly try again.

But even if his grandfather had been the intended target all along, Cole couldn't take a chance with Shawna's safety. If something happened to his grandfather, once the will was read, she would be in even more danger than she had already been.

Cole hadn't told her yet what his grandfather had done. And knowing how she felt about Xavier, he was reluctant to tell her the truth. He remembered how disillusioned and hurt she'd been when Cole had broken their engagement. Learning what Xavier had done would disillusion her, as well. She would undoubtedly be as furious as Cole had been over how the old man had tried to manipulate them both.

Shawna sat between Lars and Cole in the back seat of Xavier's town car. Astin wasn't driving. He hadn't been released from the hospital yet, but he would be soon. She'd checked on him before she had agreed to leave the hospital.

She'd wanted to stay with Xavier until he was completely recovered. Manny was posted outside the old man's hospital room along with a sheriff's deputy. Since the explosion, the police had been investigating. Their involvement had increased with the events of the day before and now with Xavier possibly being in danger.

For several reasons, he was a very important member of the community. As the owner of several businesses, he supplied most of the jobs in the area, and as a philanthropist, he contributed to all of the charities and any unfunded community project. The town needed him.

So did Shawna. Since she'd lost her parents and Cole had brought her home to meet his family, Xavier had been a constant in her life. When Cole had left for boot camp and his deployments, she and his grandfather had grown even closer in their concern and fear. "Are you sure Manny is well enough to protect him?" she asked.

"He won't have to be there long," Cooper answered her from the driver's seat. "I called in backup. One of my brother's is sending some of his bodyguards. They booked the next flight out of River City."

Would they get there soon enough to help?

"One of them should be a pilot like Cole," Lars murmured. "Then they could have gotten here faster." He was worried. From the muscle twitching in Cole's cheek just above his clenched jaw, he was worried, too.

"You really think Xavier might have been poisoned?" Cooper asked.

Shawna didn't know who he was asking until she saw his gaze focused on her in the rearview mirror. "I think it's a strong possibility," she replied,

"The sheriff said he'd have the lab rush the toxicology results," Cooper said. "We should know soon if it was poison."

"We need to find what's being poisoned," Shawna said. So that it didn't happen again.

"It can't be the food, or everyone would have gotten sick," Cooper said. "It would have to be something that only Xavier consumes."

She knew what that was. Unfortunately so did everyone else living in that house. Any one of them could have poisoned him. "I've been trying to get him to stop drinking and smoking."

"So you think it's in the cigars and alcohol?" Cooper asked.

She nodded as guilt overwhelmed her again. If she'd been doing her job, Xavier wouldn't have had the chance to sneak his scotch and cigars. Or at least not as much as he must have in order to have gotten so sick.

If she hadn't suctioned the vomit from him… If it had gotten into his lungs…

He would have aspirated and suffocated. She shuddered at the thought of losing Xavier. Sure, he was old, and he would eventually die. But he was vital now, so much more alive than many other people she knew, than most of his family.

Cole slid his arm around her shoulder, silently offering the comfort he must have realized she needed. Maybe he needed comforting, too. Xavier was his grandfather. Even as frustrated as Cole got with him, she knew he loved the old man more than any other member of his family. At least his real family.

He loved his friends like family.

"We need to get the cigars and alcohol tested," Cooper said.

"He hides them," she said.

Cooper snorted. "Yeah, right. He had a glass and a cigar in his den last night."

"But that's not where he keeps them," Shawna said. "He knows I'd find them and throw them out.

He only smoked and drank in his den because I was preoccupied."

Cole squeezed her shoulders. "It's not your fault."

He might not blame her. But Shawna blamed herself. "I saw some butts outside the back door of the garage," she said. "He has them stashed all over."

"Nikki's good at tracking things down," Cooper said. "I'll have her get everything together."

"What about Maisy?" Shawna asked. She didn't want her little girl anywhere near poison.

"Dane is watching her now," Cooper said.

"Dane?" The big, quiet guy?

Cole touched her hand. He'd probably meant to reassure her, but her pulse leaped at the brief contact. "Dane's good with kids," he said. "His girlfriend has a baby."

"My sister," Lars said. "His girlfriend is my sister." He sounded a little bitter about it. "And the baby is my nephew." Then he sighed and begrudgingly added, "And he's great with both of them."

She smiled as she began to understand the relationship between these men. Like Cooper had said, they were his family. She could see it in their brotherly comradery.

Cole squeezed her shoulders gain. "Maisy will be safe with Dane."

"And we'll be back to the estate soon," Cooper added as if he understood a parent's need to be with her child. He must be a father himself.

But Shawna's fear went far beyond separation anxiety. "Do you think she's in danger, too?" she asked Cole. "Do you think anyone knows...?"

"That she's a Bentler?" he asked. He pulled his arm out from around her as his muscular body tensed. "I think everyone knew but me."

So Maisy was in danger. If whoever was trying to poison Xavier was after the inheritance, he wouldn't want competition for the money. She turned toward Cole and tried to make him understand why she'd kept her silence. "It was better for her when no one knew for certain…"

"That she's a Bentler," he finished for her again. Then he sighed and agreed. "Yeah, it was better for her."

And for him? Did he wish he didn't know?

Then she remembered how he'd looked at the little girl as Maisy had clung to him after the gunshots had scared her. And Shawna knew, from experience when he used to look at her that way, that had been a look of love on his face. He had fallen for their daughter.

What about Shawna? Would he ever look at her that way again? Would he be able to fall for her again? Or would he never be able to forgive her for keeping the truth from him—even though it might have been keeping Maisy safe all these years?

Their daughter wasn't safe anymore. Too many people knew who she really was, that she was really Cole's daughter. A Bentler. A possible heir to billions…

"We need to hurry back," Shawna said. She needed to make certain that her daughter was all right. She never should have left her, but she'd been so worried about Xavier, about making sure that he was all right.

What about Maisy?

* * *

Guilt rose in Nikki over leaving Maisy, but at least she was with Dane. He would protect her. The minute Nikki left the room, she suspected he'd started playing with the little girl.

It wasn't like Nikki would be gone long. All she had to do was make sure she collected any of Xavier Bentler's items that might have been poisoned. She'd already been searching the house when Cooper called from the car and narrowed her search to...

Liquor and cigars.

That was what Shawna thought, according to Cooper. She'd added that the old man had to be hiding the cigars somewhere. Shawna suspected a stash in the garage since she'd found evidence of smoking outside the service door.

Nikki smiled as she thought of petite Shawna inspiring enough fear in Xavier Bentler that the billionaire had to hide his cigars from her. Shawna was so little and delicate-looking, whereas Xavier, despite his age, was still big and strong-looking. But as Nikki knew, size didn't mean anything. She suspected Shawna was strong—emotionally and mentally. She had proved that when she'd escaped the garage full of carbon monoxide.

Nikki headed from the den, through the kitchen and mudroom, to the garage.

The overhead door Shawna had smashed had already been replaced with another. A chill chased down Nikki's spine as she realized she was alone in the garage where Shawna and the chauffeur had nearly died.

But none of the cars were running today. And the lights were on, so the power had not been cut. She would be able to escape when she wanted to. She was in no danger.

Unless the killer figured out what she was looking for and wanted to cover his tracks. Then he would be after the same thing she was. She needed to find Xavier's secret stash before he could.

Shelves and pristine white cupboards lined the back wall of the long garage. She began to search among the shelves and in the cabinets. A coffee can caught her attention. It seemed out of place among the oil and gasoline containers. Why would there be a coffee can in the garage?

She reached for it and popped up the plastic top. "Gotcha…" she murmured. She'd found the cigars.

But then she heard hinges creak as a door opened. And she knew she was no longer alone.

Chapter 18

"She's gone!" Lars shouted even though Cole stood only a few feet from him. "I've searched everywhere for her, but I can't find her."

Cole wasn't as worried as his friend was. Nikki was tough and resourceful. He hadn't been lying when he'd told Shawna she was probably the best bodyguard the Payne Protection Agency had. She had to be okay.

Because she had to be okay, he felt compelled to tease his friend. "The wedding's coming up," he said. "Maybe she came to her senses and skipped out."

Lars didn't laugh like Cole had meant him to. Maybe he considered that a possibility, given the way Nikki used to feel about weddings and marriage. But when she'd fallen for his friend, all that had changed for her. There was no chance of her being a runaway bride.

"I'm kidding," Cole said. "She would never back out of marrying you." He sighed. "Guess she's not as smart as I thought she was."

"But she is," Lars said. "She is smart. She has to be okay."

Cole followed his friend as Lars walked from the den through the house. They'd searched once already and had found no sign of her. But then Cole remembered what Shawna had relayed to Nikki when Cooper had called her to secure the evidence.

"The garage," Cole said. "She was going to search the garage."

Lars cursed. "That damn garage…" He rushed through the house. The service door wasn't locked like it had been the day before. It turned easily beneath Lars's huge hand. He pushed it open and stepped inside the garage.

His hand on his holster, Cole followed him. The air was clear but for a faint trace of the fumes that had filled it the day before. That faint trace wasn't enough to have knocked out Nikki, though.

"Nikki!" Lars's deep voice cracked as he called out for his fiancée.

Even during all those dangerous missions they had carried out while Marines, Cole had never seen Lars as afraid as he was now. He'd come close, when his sister had been missing. But this was an entirely new level of fear. Cole reached out and squeezed the big guy's arm. "We'll find her."

But he worried, like Lars had to be worrying, that

they might be too late. His friend had been through so much that he'd earned the happiness he'd found with Nikki Payne. He deserved it.

Cole hoped like hell that the chance hadn't been stolen from him by a member of Cole's family. It was Cole's fault that they were even here—because Grandfather had hired Payne Protection, and Cole had insisted they come along with him.

But if Xavier hadn't hired them, both he and Shawna would be dead.

Maybe even Maisy.

"Where's Nikki?" Maisy asked the question burning inside everyone else's mind right now. While she and Dane were downstairs in the front parlor, she hadn't been near the den with the others when they weren't able to find the female bodyguard. How did she know Nikki was missing?

Shawna met Dane's worried gaze. Despite his obvious concern, he grinned at her daughter. "Hey, why are you missing Nikki?" he teased, feigning offense. "I thought you and I were having fun."

The big man sat on the floor beside the little girl, a pile of dolls and clothes between them on the antique Oriental rug. He must have brought all of Maisy's toys down to the parlor. "I've been playing Barbies with you."

Maisy smiled at him. "I know. And it's fun." Her smile slipped and she uttered a sigh that sounded almost pitying. "But you make them sound all girly. Nikki makes the Barbies tough bodyguards."

"Of course she does," Dane murmured.

Nikki was a tough bodyguard. She would be all right. Shawna was more concerned about her daughter. Would she be safe? She was so small, so young… and they were all in so much danger.

Maybe Cole was right. Maybe they needed to leave the estate. With Xavier in the hospital, she didn't need to act as his nurse anymore. He had around-the-clock staff at the hospital to monitor his recovery from whatever this *episode* proved to be. And he would have bodyguards posted outside the room to protect him from any more harm. Her patient would be a lot safer in the hospital than in his home with his greedy family. And she would be a lot safer anywhere but his home.

Where did Cole intend to bring her and their daughter? To River City? To his home?

She should have asked him before she'd refused to even consider it. She needed to talk to him about it, about their entire situation. That conversation would have to wait until Nikki was found.

Then she heard it—the faint wail of a siren. Fear coursed through her that Nikki had been found. And wasn't okay.

A curse slipped through Dane's lips, but he muffled it enough that Maisy might have missed it. Shawna hadn't missed the oath or the look of fear on his face, though. The sirens grew louder, and red-and-white lights flashed behind the blinds at the front window.

The little girl jumped up and pulled open the blinds to peer out at the driveway. "It's an ambulance!"

Oh, God, Nikki had been hurt. Why hadn't Cole

come for her? Maybe Shawna could have treated her until the paramedics arrived. But nobody even stood on the driveway to meet the ambulance. Hadn't someone called for it?

A paramedic opened up the back doors and wheeled out a stretcher. There was already a body on it, one that squirmed around and tried to sit up and bark out orders. Probably for cigars.

Even while her heart warmed with love for the old man, she felt a stab of fear—for him and for her and Maisy and Cole. It wasn't safe for him to come back here, not if someone had really tried to poison him.

"It's Grampa X," Maisy said with delight. "He's home."

"He's stubborn," Shawna murmured.

Dane met her gaze and nodded. "But at least the ambulance isn't for..."

Nikki. But that didn't mean she didn't need it. Where the hell was Nikki? Everyone was searching for her, which was why Shawna was with Maisy. Dane was protecting them both while Cole, Lars and Cooper looked for Nikki. But now she needed to help settle Xavier into his room.

"I need to go out there and make sure he's okay," Shawna said. She could not imagine why the doctor would have released him. Then again, knowing Xavier Bentler as long as she did, she could well imagine why. Xavier, in his indomitable way, had insisted, and the doctor had been unable to resist.

Dane shook his head. "You can't go out there. You're supposed to stay in here at least until the others return."

Manny jumped down from the back of the ambulance and walked beside the stretcher. He wasn't alone. Another man stood on the other side of the stretcher—with his bushy beard and unkempt appearance, Shawna wasn't certain if he was a bodyguard or...

"Who's that?" she asked Dane, who stood at the window, too.

"He's one of Parker's team," Dane replied. "They're all former vice cops. They're good—if a little rough around the edges."

"You'll stay with Maisy?" she asked. She didn't want her daughter being protected by someone a little rough around the edges.

But then maybe all of Cooper's team were, as well. They had the short, military-style haircuts, but they had an edge to them, too. Cole even had it—the edge that hadn't been there before. They'd seen and done things that had changed them.

How much had Cole changed? Was he really the man she'd loved?

Or had she misplaced her heart by giving it to him once again?

Nikki's lungs burned from exertion, and her heart pounded like mad. She'd never been as spent as she was now—except maybe after some of her marathon lovemaking sessions with Lars.

Despite her frustration, a smile stole over her lips. Then she let out a little gasp as an enormous shadow stepped into her path, blocking her from the sunlight. But his hair was such a pale blond that he was nearly as bright as the sun—except for his face, that was dark with a glower.

"Do you think this is funny?" Lars demanded.

"What?" she asked. "What are you talking about?" She didn't find her current situation funny at all. She was pissed—damn pissed that the killer had gotten the jump on her.

"You scared me half to death!" he said. He scooped her up in his arms and pulled her close to his massive chest. His heart beat frantically against hers. "We couldn't find you. And I was so damn worried something had happened to you." He put up his hand to cup the back of her head in his palm, and she cried out as he hit the bump.

He started cursing all over again. Then he yelled out, "I found her, but she's hurt."

Within seconds, her brother and Cole appeared at Lars's side, their faces tense with concern. "I am totally fine," she assured them all. "I'm just angry."

"You have a huge bump," Lars said. He gently ran his fingers over the goose egg on the back of her head. Her hair was sticky with the blood that had oozed from the wound, and his fingers tangled in it.

She winced and sucked in a breath at the pain. "I had the cigars," she told them. "I found them in a coffee can in one of the cabinets in the garage. I put down my gun to open the can, and someone got the jump on me." Once she'd heard the door creak open, she'd grabbed for her weapon. She hadn't drawn it fast enough.

"Did you see who it was?" Cole asked.

She cursed herself for not being more aware and shook her head. "No. I got hit from behind."

"Did you lose consciousness?" Lars asked.

She closed her eyes and struggled to remember. "I don't think so. I saw stars for a little bit, and by the time I could focus again, I saw someone heading out the back door." It had just been a hazy shadow really; she hadn't been able to focus right away. "So I chased after him."

Lars groaned and sarcastically remarked, "Of course you did."

"Of course I did," she agreed. "That's my job." She looked beyond Lars for the moment to direct her frustration at Cole and Cooper. "And your jobs are to protect Shawna and Maisy. I'm fine. Please, get back to your posts."

Cooper and Cole studied her face for a moment before they nodded and headed back toward the house.

She breathed a sigh of relief. She would have felt terrible had something happened to Shawna or Maisy because they'd been preoccupied looking for her. She wriggled in Lars's arms, trying to regain her feet, so that she could continue her search for the stolen cigars.

But Lars tightened his grasp on her. She looked up into his face and saw that he had been really worried. Regret struck her heart. "I'm sorry," she said.

"You weren't answering your cell, and we couldn't find you." He shuddered.

She patted her pocket and realized it was missing. "I must have lost it somewhere." Probably when she'd fallen in the gardens. It had taken a little while for her to focus and regain her balance. "I didn't mean to worry you."

He nodded, and his throat moved as if he were struggling to swallow his emotion. "I love you so much. I don't know what I'd do if I lost you forever."

She wound her arm around his neck and pulled his head down for a kiss. "You are not going to lose me," she promised him. "Ever."

He kissed her deeply before pulling back to expel a ragged breath. "I know. I know that you're tough as hell and can take care of yourself."

Her heart swelled with even more love for him. And she'd already thought she couldn't love him more than she already did. "I love you, and I can't wait to marry you."

His pale eyes widened in surprise. He knew how she'd once felt about marriage. But the minute she'd met him, all that had changed. He had changed everything for her. She couldn't imagine losing him either. But he was as tough and independent as she was.

They didn't have to worry about losing each other. They only had to worry about doing their jobs well and making sure their friend didn't lose anyone he loved either. Like his grandfather or his daughter or the woman he still loved.

Or his own life…

Chapter 19

Cole stared at the people gathered in his grandfather's room around the bed. This was his family. And one of them was a killer.

Who?

He couldn't tell just by looking at them. Some of them actually looked concerned over what had happened to the old man. They might just be faking that. Cole studied each of them intently, looking for any flash of remorse. No, not remorse. A person greedy enough to kill a relative for an inheritance wasn't capable of remorse. He needed to look for disappointment. Whoever poisoned the old man had to be damn disappointed that the attempt failed.

His grandfather had had three sons. Cole's father was dead, but his uncles, Ronald and Lawrence, were alive and bitterly resentful. Both were divorced, and they each had a couple of kids. Cole's cousins Bobby and Reggie were Uncle Ronald's sons, and the twins belonged to Lawrence. Every one of them was bitterly resentful despite living off Grandfather. Of course, Xavier made them work in his business, not that any of them did much to earn their extravagant keep.

Then there was Cole's mother, who'd moved in with Grandfather after Cole's dad died and disinherited her. And when Tiffani had remarried, her husband had been welcomed into the fold.

His stepfather, Jeffrey Inman, was probably about as different from Cole's father as he could possibly be, probably as different as Emery Little had been from Cole. Jeff was quiet and conservative and generally well liked, although Grandfather had never been a big fan. He naturally mistrusted the quiet ones. He must have loved having Manny as his bodyguard at the hospital. And that was where he should have stayed.

Stubborn old fool.

Had Grandfather liked Emery Little? Cole had never asked him. He hadn't really wanted to know anything about the man Shawna had married. And now he would never have the chance. He felt bad—about Little, and about his stepfather.

Cole didn't know Jeffrey that well either. He'd been off on a mission when his mother had met the man, apparently through AA meetings although they weren't supposed to have disclosed that, and then married him. Unlike Cole's father, Jeffrey Inman had fallen hard and fast for his mother. He seemed to adore her.

Like Emery must have adored Shawna. Why else would he have married her and claimed another man's child as his?

Cole couldn't blame him. She was a loving, generous woman. She bustled around his grandfather's room, totally focused on the old man's comfort. She was a natural caregiver.

Was that what last night had been about? Cole had saved her life so she'd rewarded him with pleasure? She'd always had such gratitude—even as a little kid, when he'd helped her deal with bullies. Back then she'd just tried to give him her lunch and made him *thank you for being my friend* cards.

How could one of these people, one of his family, want to hurt her? Didn't they know how he felt about her?

Then he noticed that they were watching him watch her, and he knew that they knew.

Maybe that was why she was in danger? Not just because she stood between his grandfather and death but because she was an easy way to get back at Cole for inheriting his father's entire estate. And if they knew about the changes to his grandfather's will...

"I need to talk to the old man," Cole told the others. Yet they all just stood there, watching him with hostility. Even his mother.

She was angry with him for some reason. He wasn't sure what he'd done besides reminding her too much of his father, and he couldn't change that. He was too much like his father, more even than he had known. But unlike his father, he would make sure nothing happened to his first and only love. He would protect Shawna. He'd thought that was what his grandfather would do, as well.

But the old man had disappointed him. He never should have come back to this house.

"I need to talk to him alone," Cole said.

Shawna glanced at him before she turned toward his resentful relatives. Then she put her hands on her hips and faced them all down as if she was six foot instead of barely five. "Xavier needs his rest," she told them. "You all need to leave."

And remarkably, they listened to her. Cole's stepfather opened the door and held it for the others. And as he held it, a small person rushed inside and jumped onto the bed with his grandfather.

Xavier was tired but not so weak that he didn't immediately close his arms around the little girl and pull her close to his chest—to his heart. She'd stolen it, probably years ago, just as she'd stolen Cole's.

"Grampa X, are you all right?" she asked.

He patted her head. "Yes, my darling. I'm fine. I just ate something I shouldn't have."

Poison. It must have been in the cigars. Why else would someone have taken such a risk to get them away from Nikki? Had the killer been worried they'd left prints on something—the coffee can, the cigar bands?

"Did you eat too many cookies?" the little girl asked the old man.

Xavier laughed, although it wasn't quite as hearty as usual. The stress and the poison had taken their toll. He shouldn't have left the hospital. "There is no such thing as too many cookies," he told her with a grin. Then he lowered his voice and whispered not quite softly enough to keep Cole and Shawna from hearing him, "You could go get me a few from the kitchen."

"No cookies," Shawna admonished them both. "Grampa needs sleep." She took her little girl's hand and guided Maisy off the bed. She gave Cole a pointed glance as she passed him on her way to where Dane waited in the doorway. His friend would protect them both, but the job wasn't his alone. He had backup.

Cole needed to eliminate the reason they needed protection, though. He needed to find Emery Little's killer. Once the door closed, he turned on his grandfather.

"What the hell were you thinking?" he asked. "Why didn't you stay in the hospital?"

"I didn't think it was safe," Xavier said.

"For whom?" Cole asked. "Because it certainly isn't safer for Shawna and Maisy. I could have taken them home—"

"Home?"

"To River City," Cole said. "That's home now." More home than this estate or this town had ever been for him. "I could have protected them better there."

"So take them," Xavier urged him.

Cole shook his head. He already knew an argument would be pointless. "There's no way Shawna's leaving you."

"I'll fire her."

"If I thought that would make a difference, I'd tell you to do it," Cole said. "But she'd still refuse to leave you." And he understood why. Xavier had stood by her, even after Cole had broken their engagement, Xavier had not abandoned her like everyone else in her life. Cole was grateful for that.

He'd made a horrible mistake when he'd broken their engagement. He hadn't protected her. He'd hurt her.

Xavier groaned.

Cole moved closer to the bed. "Are you all right?"

The old man shook his head. "No. I'm a damn fool," he berated himself. "I made a horrible mess of things."

Cole couldn't lie. "You did."

"I probably shouldn't have survived," Xavier said. "At my age, it'd be no great loss. I'm old."

But vibrant and aware. "Now you're talking like a damn fool," Cole said. "Nobody wants you dead."

Xavier snorted. "Somebody certainly does."

Cole reached for the old man's hand and clasped it in his. He offered a reassuring squeeze. "Not me. Not Shawna and certainly not that little girl."

Xavier sucked in a breath. "I'm sorry, Cole. I didn't mean to put you and your family in danger."

He'd just meant to put them back together. Cole understood the reason behind his manipulations. Unfortunately, the killer would not.

"But if something happens to me, you and Shawna will be in more danger."

Cole sighed. "I can't believe you changed your will to that."

Xavier offered an unrepentant grin. "That you

and Shawna inherit everything but only if you get married."

"It's crazy," Cole told him. "And it's never going to happen."

"Why not?" Xavier asked. "You can't tell me it's because you don't love her. You do—you loved her from the first moment you saw her and you've never stopped."

It was because Cole loved her that he couldn't marry her. Loving her would put her in too much danger.

Cole snorted. "I didn't figure you for this romantic nonsense of soul mates and all that. You've been married three times. You must have never had a Natalie." Or a Shawna.

Grandfather sighed, and he suddenly looked every one of his eighty-six years.

"There's a story in that sigh," Cole remarked. "Who was she?"

Grandfather shook his head. "She was never mine. She was married to my old partner, Albert Coleman."

"Coleman," he said. "That's who you named my father after."

"And you're named after your father." Xavier settled back against his pillows.

"He died, right?" Cole asked. "Years ago?"

Xavier nodded. "Heart attack in the office one night. I worked him too hard."

"Was that what she thought?"

"Edith?" Xavier nodded again. "I think so. She wanted nothing to do with me. She sold me what she'd inherited of the company and took off. I don't even know where she moved."

"Then how do you know she was your soul mate?" Cole asked.

Xavier pressed a fist against his heart. "Because I felt it every time I saw her." He sighed again, wearily. "My heart belonged to her."

But she had belonged to another. Just like Shawna had once belonged to Emery Little. But like Albert Coleman, Emery was dead now. Would Shawna let Cole back into her heart? Or did it belong to a dead man?

Shawna had waited all day for the fight with Cole. The one where he once again demanded that she and Maisy pack up and go to some safe house and she refused. But that argument never came.

She barely even saw him. She stayed close to Xavier, making sure he was well enough to have been released from the hospital. She suspected he'd used his wealth and influence to get the medical clearance to go home. But she was happier having him under her care again. And after what had nearly happened to him, she was extra diligent.

She had no idea where Cole even was. Had he been removed from the assignment? But when she tucked Maisy into bed for the night, he appeared.

Maisy hopped up and declared, "Rematch!"

"Rematch?" Shawna asked. "What?"

"Checkers," Cole said. "She beat me at checkers several times today."

He'd been with their daughter?

Maisy laughed and shook her head. "He beat me," she said. "That's why I need a rematch."

"We're tied right now," Cole told her. "So we can start tomorrow fresh."

Shawna's heart warmed that he was making plans to play with their daughter. The little girl mattered to him. Did Shawna?

"And once you get a good night's sleep, I'm sure you will beat me every game tomorrow," he assured her.

Maisy smiled but didn't deny it as she settled back against her pillows. Cole leaned over her bed, and she wound her thin little arms around his neck and kissed his cheek. "Good night, Daddy," she murmured sleepily. "I'll see you tomorrow."

"Good night, sweetheart," he murmured back, his voice gruff as if emotion choked him. He kissed her forehead and pulled back.

The look on his handsome face as he stared down at the little girl had Shawna closing her eyes against the wave of tears rushing over her. She'd made a horrible mistake—one that it was six years too late to undo.

When she opened her eyes again, he was gone from the room and Maisy was already asleep. She drew in a deep breath before she stepped out into the hall. A new guard stood outside Maisy's door. Shawna should be relieved that he didn't look at her with the same judgment as Cole's friends had. But she found herself more comfortable with them protecting her daughter. She knew they would willingly give up their lives for their friend's daughter. She wasn't so sure about this man; he wasn't as big as Cole's friends. But then Nikki wasn't big either. Just fierce.

The man was astute though. He assured her, "I will keep her safe."

She expelled the breath she'd been holding and murmured, "Thank you," as she passed him. She wasn't certain which room to use, Cole's or the one in which she'd nearly been killed. The door and the jamb had been repaired. She hesitated a moment, her heart beating in her throat, before she pushed open the door and stepped inside.

And like that night when she'd awakened chilled and frightened, she saw a shadow looming in the dark. Before she could utter the scream burning her throat, a light flipped on, and she identified the shadow as Cole.

She pressed a hand to her madly pounding heart. "You scared me!"

"I'm sorry," he said. "I was just making sure the windows were locked."

She was glad now that she'd chosen her room since he obviously hadn't intended for her to share his again. Her face flushed with heat as she thought of the night before, how they'd made love. Well, she'd made love because she still loved him. Could he love her again after finding out she'd kept his daughter from him for six years?

"Thank you." She waited but he didn't leave.

Instead he stepped closer to her and brushed his fingertips over her cheek. "You look exhausted," he said.

She was—too exhausted to fight her feelings for

him. She slid her arms around his waist and leaned her head against his muscular chest. She needed him. Needed his strength, his warmth, his forgiveness.

She didn't ask for any of those things, though. She didn't ask for anything.

But he gave her his passion. Lowering his head to hers, he kissed her deeply. His mouth moved over hers, his lips nibbling and clinging to hers before his tongue slid between them. He made love to her mouth. Then he lifted and carried her to the bed.

And he made love to her body.

He undressed her slowly and kissed and caressed every inch of her. He swept his tongue across each nipple before closing his lips around it and pulling it into his mouth. The sensation raced through her, and she cried out with pleasure. But it wasn't enough. He was driving her out of her mind with desire. His fingertips traced every curve of her body, as if he were committing them to memory.

Maybe he was.

She could still remember that last time they'd made love six years ago—how thorough and insatiable he'd been. He must have known then that it would be the last time. She hadn't. Or she would have paid even more attention.

Like she did now. She kissed him back, tried to unclasp his belt, but he caught her hands and pulled them away. And he continued to give her pleasure as he moved down her body. His tongue teased her before slipping into her core.

She whimpered as she came. But it wasn't enough

to relieve the tension and the emptiness inside her. Only he could fill her.

Finally he stripped off his clothes. Then he joined her in the madness, joining their bodies, filling that emptiness that had ached for him for so many years.

They moved instinctively—their rhythm matching perfectly—as he thrust and she arched, meeting him each time. Passion claimed her, the tension building inside her until it was unbearable.

The tension broke as an orgasm shuddered through her. She bit her lip to hold back her scream of pleasure and the declaration of love that burned the back of her throat. She couldn't tell him how she felt for so many reasons. Most especially because she didn't think he could ever return her feelings again.

While he made love to her, he didn't love her. He couldn't—not after what she had done.

That ornery old bastard...

How could someone that old be so damned resilient? The poison should have killed him by now. Of course he hadn't been getting that much of it—thanks to his damn ever-vigilant nurse.

But maybe it was good that he hadn't died yet.

Thanks to the little girl's eavesdropping, everybody had learned that ornery old bastard had secretly changed his will just like his son had.

Coleman hadn't died in vain, though. He had deserved to die, had deserved to give his life for the one he'd taken. But it had been unfortunate that his estate had gone to Cole. It had been even more unfortunate that Cole had survived all those years he'd been a Marine. Everything would have been so much easier if he was dead and not around to play hero to his ex-girlfriend and his grandfather.

At least Xavier, unlike his son, had put a condition on Cole inheriting. He had to marry Shawna. Well, he couldn't marry a dead woman. Nor could he get married if he was dead.

One of them had to die. Maybe it would be best to kill them both—just to make sure that this time the inheritance was bequeathed to the rightful heirs.

Chapter 20

Whht the hell kind of bodyguard was he?

Cole couldn't believe he had fallen asleep. Of course, he hadn't slept at all the night before. But he'd been on duty that night and last night, as well. He was supposed to protect Shawna, not put her in more danger.

He'd put himself in danger, too, and not just physically. He was in danger of falling even more deeply in love with her than he'd already been. So when he'd awakened to find her clasped in his arms, her head on his chest, he'd panicked more so than if he'd discovered another intruder in the room. His heart pounded frantically, so hard and loud that he was surprised it didn't awaken her. He was able to ease her away to a pillow with only a slight murmur of protest from her.

She had to be as exhausted as he'd been. She'd lost her husband and nearly her own life a couple of times. And his grandfather…

If something happened to the old man, she would be devastated. Cole had to make sure nothing happened to Xavier—for Shawna and Maisy and for himself. He couldn't lose the one family member he trusted. Not that he had any reason to trust Xavier after the stunts he'd pulled.

Changing his will…

Hopefully no one found out about that or Shawna and Cole would be in even more danger. He dressed quickly and slipped out into the hall. And was nearly shot as a gun cocked and the barrel pointed at him.

He lifted his hands. "Hey, easy…"

This man with his bushy beard and long hair was one of Parker Payne's bodyguards. Most of them were former cops Parker had worked with while he'd been in the vice unit with the River City Police Department. Unfortunately, they all looked as if they might have picked up a few vices from all the years they'd been undercover.

Cole would have preferred it if Logan had sent his bodyguards. They were all Payne family members and unequivocally trustworthy—unlike Cole's family, who could not be trusted at all. One of them was a killer.

Which one?

Another door opened off the hall. Cole grabbed the bodyguard's hand before he could draw his gun again and terrify the little girl who rushed out of her bedroom. Nikki followed her, and she drew up short as she nearly ran into Shawna's guard. "Hey."

The man nodded at her but that was it. He wasn't a talker, which was fine with Cole. He heard enough talking from Manny.

Apparently his daughter was chatty, too, because words poured out of her. "Daddy! Daddy! I was telling Nikki that you're going to marry Mommy soon."

Nikki nodded and studied him through narrowed eyes, probably trying to determine if he'd lost his mind. "That's what she's been telling me."

"Where would you get that idea?" he asked as he lifted the little girl into his arms.

"Grampa," she said. "I heard him saying that you gotta marry Mommy for his heritage."

"Heritage?" Nikki asked, with an arched brow.

Inheritance. "Grampa told you about that?" Had the old man lost his mind completely? Maybe the poison had affected him more than Cole thought.

The little girl's face flushed pink with embarrassment. "I heard him telling you 'bout it."

She must have been eavesdropping outside his grandfather's bedroom. Alarm had his every muscle tensing. "Did anyone else overhear that?" he asked.

She shrugged. "Maybe Dane. He was with me."

He didn't have to worry about Dane telling anyone. He was as quiet as Manny was chatty. "Did *you* tell anyone besides Nikki what you overheard?" he asked.

If the killer knew…

She looked down into his face, and she must have seen his concern because she tensed. "I—I told

Miss Tiffani." Her brow puckered. "Should I call her Grandma?"

Cole realized that she probably already had. And of every member of his family, his mother was the last person with whom Maisy should have shared what she'd heard. Like Manny, Cole's mother couldn't keep a secret, at least she certainly hadn't been able to when she'd been drinking. And despite her AA attendance, Cole was skeptical as to whether she'd ever really stopped. She was still given to outbursts where she shared too much information. Surely she had already gossiped with everyone around the breakfast table.

Now his whole damn family—the killer among them—knew for certain that Maisy was his child and that Grandfather had changed his will.

Damn it!

How would he protect them now?

Shawna had awakened the minute Cole slipped out of bed. It had been obvious that he hadn't wanted to wake her so she'd pretended to stay asleep. When he left the room, she'd dressed quickly, which was good because she'd heard the voices in the hall. She hadn't been able to discern words, though—just the high, lilting voice of her daughter and the deep voice of her lover.

Of Cole…

She couldn't face him again, not after last night, after she'd thrown herself at him. She waited until she no longer heard his voice before she opened the door to the hall.

"See, she's awake!" Maisy told Nikki who smiled at Shawna over the little girl's head.

"Yes, I'm awake." She had slept in longer than she normally would have, longer than she should have. She'd felt so safe and protected in Cole's arms. Crazy, considering nobody had ever hurt her like he had. "I need to check on Grampa X," she told her daughter. "Then after we eat breakfast, we can play."

Maisy's bottom lip began to quiver and tears pooled in her eyes. It wasn't like her to pout when she didn't immediately get her way. But she hadn't actually even asked Shawna to play. Cole was the one with whom she had wanted to play checkers again.

Shawna pulled the little girl into her arms and hugged her closely. "What's wrong, sweetheart?" she asked, her heart breaking as tears trailed down her daughter's face. "Why are you crying?"

Nikki lowered her head and bit her bottom lip, as if she was tempted to cry, too.

"I think my new daddy's mad at me," Maisy said.

"Of course he isn't," Shawna assured her even as she flinched over Maisy calling him her *new* daddy. He wasn't new. He was her real dad. Guilt weighed heavily on her for all the years they'd missed out on being with each other.

"Is he mad at you?" Maisy asked.

"Why would you ask that?" Shawna wondered.

Maisy was so intuitive that she might have picked up on Cole's anger with her, his resentment over the choices Shawna had made—to marry another man and let that man claim his daughter.

Or maybe she'd overheard something...

"Because he doesn't want to marry you," Maisy said.

Shawna sucked in a breath of shock. Why was the little girl talking about marriage?

"He never said that," Nikki cautioned her.

"But he was mad about what Grampa X did," Maisy said.

What had Grampa X done? She braced herself and turned to Nikki. "What did he do?"

"You should really talk to Cole about it," the female bodyguard said. She wouldn't meet Shawna's eyes.

Oh, God, what had he done? Was it why Maisy was talking about Cole marrying her? Or was that the little girl's own wish—for her parents to marry?

"Where is Cole?" Shawna asked.

"He's talking to Cooper," Nikki replied.

Was he asking to be removed from the assignment? He'd made it clear six years ago that he didn't want to marry Shawna. While she suspected—while she hoped—that he may have only broken their engagement to protect her, she didn't know that for certain. And even if he had, it didn't mean he would ever want to marry her now after what she'd done, after she'd kept his daughter from him.

Now that daughter had more tears spilling from her deep blue eyes and pouring down her cheeks. "I don't want to lose my new daddy, too."

Shawna tightened her embrace. "You're not going

to lose him," she said. She hoped she wasn't making a promise she couldn't keep.

Cole was only doing his job. And maybe right now he was getting out of that job and out of her and Maisy's lives. He'd never said he wanted a relationship with his child. Or with her...

Cooper shook his head. "Absolutely not."

"I wasn't asking permission," Cole said.

And Cooper realized that his employee hadn't even asked for this meeting. Cole had found Cooper downstairs and pulled him into his grandfather's den, breaking through the crime scene tape. The room had already been searched by the police and by Nikki the day before. Whatever evidence had been there was already collected.

"Did you forget who's the boss?" Cooper asked.

He should have taken Cole off this assignment despite his objections. But given how Cooper felt about his wife Tanya and their own children, he understood there was no way he could have gotten Cole away from his daughter and his ex-fiancée while they were in danger. He hadn't left Tanya's side when she'd needed protection. Hell, he hated leaving now, even when she didn't need protection.

He was so damn desperate to wrap up this assignment just so he could get home to Tanya and their babies that he was tempted to go along with Cole's crazy plan. But it was too risky.

"I know you're the boss," Cole assured him. "But I know this family. You don't."

Cooper was glad that he didn't. The old man was

the only Bentler, besides Cole, that he actually liked. The others were all self-absorbed, selfish and spoiled. Not like his family at all. Nobody in the Payne family was any of those things. After meeting the Bentlers, Cooper had never appreciated his family more than he did now.

"That's why *I* needed to come up with the plan," Cole continued.

But what he was suggesting... Cooper shook his head. "I'm not sure how this even flushes out the killer." Although, he suspected Cole was less worried about the risk to himself than keeping Shawna and Maisy safe. And the only way to really do that was to catch the killer and make sure he could never harm them.

"I have to do it," Cole insisted. "It might be the only way to protect everyone."

Maybe Cooper hadn't understood exactly how the plan was supposed to work, because he was certain that someone was going to get hurt. And it wasn't just that sixth sense he'd inherited from his mother. He didn't need to be clairvoyant to see that this plan wasn't going to turn out well.

"This whole thing could backfire on you—badly," Cooper warned.

Cole might lose his chance at happiness.

Forever.

Chapter 21

Cole drew in a deep breath before stepping into the dining room where all of his family had gathered around the long table. He'd missed breakfast but then so had most of them.

His cousins, although older than him, stayed up late and partied like they were still in college. They weren't too concerned about getting to the office on time since their fathers weren't all that concerned either. His uncles made their own hours, as well. Even after their father's heart attack, they apparently hadn't stepped in to help out any more than the very little they already did.

But his grandfather hadn't built his billion-dollar empire by accident. He was smart enough to have hired other people he could trust since he couldn't trust any members of his own damn family.

Cole looked away from them, too disgusted to study their faces for signs of guilt. He knew he wasn't going to find remorse in any of them.

He focused on his mother instead. Since getting pregnant with him during her internship at his father's business, Tiffani Bentler-Inman had never worked beyond helping out with Shawna at the high school, coaching the cheerleaders. His stepfather had worked, though. Jeff was retired from the military. Like Cole, he never talked about his service.

Everyone glanced up as he entered the room, as if surprised to see him. He had pretty much been trying to avoid them all since taking this assignment, so he understood their surprise. "I guess by now you've all heard about Grandfather changing his will," he said.

Uncle Lawrence snorted. He had the Bentler blue eyes and blond hair but his had thinned so much he was nearly bald. "So what—you've come in here to rub it in?"

Yes, they'd all heard.

"I don't want his money," Cole said. He wanted the old man alive and well. If only Xavier could live forever.

"Just like you didn't want your father's," Uncle Ronald sniped at him.

Cole wished his father could have lived forever, too, or at least long enough for the two of them to spend more time together. Coleman Bentler had always been so busy, but maybe that was because of Natalie. If he hadn't stayed occupied, he would have focused on what had happened to her—because of him.

"I didn't want my father's money," Cole insisted.

"So why didn't you spread any of it around?" one of the bleached-blonde twins asked. He couldn't tell who was Tori and who was Lori.

"I couldn't," he said.

His father had been very specific in his will, which had included a video message to Cole. He hadn't wanted any other family member to ever touch his money. What about Maisy? She hadn't existed yet when his father had died, but Cole suspected he would have loved the little girl—just like Xavier did.

Just like Cole did.

He had to do this for her, to keep her and her mother safe, he reminded himself. As per his wishes, Nikki had taken the little girl out to the gardens, well out of earshot of this conversation. He couldn't risk Maisy overhearing what he was about to say. She would hate him.

Shawna and her bodyguard walked into the dining room. Cole had requested that Manny bring her to the meeting. She needed to hear what he said and she needed to believe it—just as she had when he'd broken their engagement. Hurting her that time had nearly killed him.

He hated that he had to hurt her again. Last time, he'd thought he was doing what was best for her. He could see now that he might have been wrong. But this time...

He had no choice. He wasn't just trying to protect

her heart and her happiness. He was trying to protect her life and their daughter's life.

"I don't want Grandfather's money," Cole repeated.

Cousin Bobby shook his head. "You expect us to believe that?"

He wasn't expecting it; he was counting on it. Otherwise his plan would fail and he would have hurt Shawna for no reason. It had to work. He had to make them believe him.

"There's no way I would touch his money," Cole insisted, "because of the condition he put on inheriting."

Uncle Lawrence snorted again. "That you have to marry the woman you've always loved? Yeah, some condition."

Cole mimicked his uncle's snort of derision. "Love?"

"Don't deny it," his mother said as she looked from him to Shawna, who had gone deathly pale. "You've already hurt her so badly. Don't hurt her again!"

"Of course *you* would defend her," Cole said. "She did the same thing you did. But at least you were honest with my father. She hid my child from me."

Shawna flinched as if his words struck her like blows. But she didn't defend herself. She said nothing at all.

Had Manny warned her? But while Manny struggled to keep little secrets, he kept the big ones, the ones that mattered, the life-and-death secrets. So, no, he wouldn't have told her about Cole's plan. He wouldn't have betrayed their years of friendship for a woman he didn't completely trust himself.

"And for that, I will never forgive her," Cole said. He forced a bitter chuckle before adding, "And I will damn well never marry her."

"Not even for Grandfather's millions?" one of his cousins goaded him. One of the damn twins again.

"Sure, right," the other twin skeptically chimed in. Besides looking exactly alike, the two were nearly as inseparable as conjoined twins. They could have been working together this entire time.

"I don't need Grandfather's millions," Cole said. "I have my inheritance from my father that I haven't even touched yet." Except for the ring he'd bought Shawna. That was the only thing on which he'd spent his father's money, knowing that he would have approved. His father had liked Shawna.

Why had he never told him about Natalie? Had it been too painful for him to talk about? Cole could understand that. He hadn't discussed Shawna very much with his friends. The one who knew the best how he'd felt about her—how he still felt about her— was Manny.

His friend stared at him now, and Cole could feel his disapproval. Like Cooper, he hadn't liked the plan at all. Cole didn't either, but it was the only way.

"So if something happens to Grandfather, it looks like that inheritance will remain in limbo forever— because I will *never* meet his conditions."

Shawna stood frozen in the doorway. Or maybe Manny was holding her in place. While he hadn't agreed with Cole's plan, he had committed to helping him carry it out.

His mother rushed up to him. "What are you doing?" she asked, and she stared at him as if she'd never seen him before. Cole suspected she never truly had. Every time she looked at him, she only ever saw his father. A large reason why they had never been close. "Why are you acting this way?"

"You're the one who told me I'm like my father," he reminded her.

She knew all too well that his father had never forgiven her. Maybe he hadn't forgiven himself for Natalie's death either.

Cole knew that if something happened to Shawna, he would never forgive himself. But nothing would happen to her—if his plan worked. He had to make certain that it worked.

"He didn't need family and neither do I," he said. "The only reason I'm here is because of Grandfather's manipulations. So I am damn well not going to let that old bastard succeed at his sick little game."

Shawna's mouth fell open on a silent gasp as if he'd punched her. Then she turned on her heel and ran from the room.

Pain gripped his heart. He'd hurt her, just like he had six years ago. He'd seen then how devastated she'd been. That was probably why she'd kept Maisy from him. His plan had gone too well. He'd wanted to make sure she wouldn't mourn him if he hadn't survived his mission. But he had survived.

He was more concerned about now. Would this plan work, and would he survive if it did?

* * *

Shawna had wondered if Cole would ever forgive her. Now she had her answer. After they'd made love—twice—she'd let herself hope for a future with him. But he had denied that future six years ago.

And now he'd denied it again.

He would never forgive her for keeping Maisy from him. She couldn't blame him. Had the situation been reversed, she might not have been able to forgive him either.

If only she had listened to Emery. He'd thought she should tell Cole the truth. He'd even tried to reunite them when he'd called Cole that time. But Cole had refused to talk to him. And he apparently refused to accept her apology now.

She'd run from the dining room so quickly that she'd shaken off her bodyguard. Someone else had followed, though. A hand grasped her arm and whirled her around in the kitchen.

She expected—she hoped—it was Cole to assure her he was lying. Instead it was his mother. While Shawna proudly blinked back tears, Tiffani let hers roll down her beautiful face.

"I'm sorry," she told Shawna as if any of this was her fault.

"Why?" Shawna asked. "I'm the one who caused this." If only she'd told him the truth six years ago.

"I thought I raised him to be a better man than his father," Tiffani said. "But I think he might be worse."

Shawna shook her head, refusing to believe that.

Tiffani patted her cheek. "I'm sorry," she said

again. "This is so hard for you. I didn't really love his father." She'd made no secret of that. Everyone knew that she'd only married Coleman for his money. But he'd made her pay for her greed; she had suffered. That was why she'd started drinking so much, to drown her sorrows.

Tiffani continued, "But I can see that you really loved Cole."

She had. She did. She really loved him and that love would never be returned.

"I—I need to get away for a little while," Shawna said. She was reeling from the pain Cole's cold words had inflicted. "I need to breathe…"

Tiffani let go of her arm. "Of course, go," she urged. They had become friends, years ago, while they both worked with the high school cheerleaders. Despite the mistakes she had made, Tiffani had become a mentor to many of them. *A case of do what I say, not what I did*

Shawna glanced behind her and could see Manny's shadow falling across the floor from where he stood just outside the kitchen doorway. In order to breathe, she needed to get away from him—away from Cole's friends and from all the damn Payne Protection bodyguards.

After what Cole had said, she would no longer need protection. The killer, whoever he was, would not believe she posed any threat to his inheritance. She hadn't even known his grandfather had changed his will.

She needed to talk to Xavier. But she wasn't

going to be able to do that with bodyguards looming around them both.

She leaned closer to Tiffani and whispered, "I need your help."

"Son of a bitch," Manny murmured. He stood in the middle of the library that was empty of everyone but Emery Little's urn of ashes. He'd searched everywhere—to no avail.

"What'd you call me?" a deep voice asked. There was a trace of amusement in it. Manny knew that wouldn't last when he turned to face his friend.

Cole tensed as he glanced around the empty library. "Where is she?"

Manny shook his head. "I don't know." He'd checked everywhere for her.

"What happened?" Cole asked.

"You saw her run out of the dining room," Manny reminded him. He regretted saying that when his friend flinched with regret.

Cole hadn't wanted to hurt her. But how could he think his plan would do anything else? He must have known that what he said would devastate her.

"You were supposed to stick with her," Cole said.

And now Manny flinched. "I tried. But your mother got in my way. By the time I got around her, Shawna was completely out of my sight."

Cole cursed.

"I don't know where she went," Manny admitted miserably. "I looked everywhere for her." Twice. Where the hell could she be?

But that wasn't even the question burning the

hottest in Manny's mind. Why the hell had Cooper signed off on such a plan? Of course, the Payne Protection Agency wasn't beyond enacting a risky plan to flush out the threat to whoever they were protecting. But this plan wouldn't flush out the killer. It just gave him a motive to stop trying to kill Shawna.

But if they never learned who the killer was, Cole and Shawna could never be together.

So had Cole come up with this plan to protect Shawna or to protect himself from the risk of falling for her again?

Chapter 22

Cole buried his fury and forced a smile. But it was for Maisy's sake, not his mother's. Tiffani Bentler-Inman sat on a bench in the garden with his daughter on her lap.

His mother had helped Shawna shake off her protection duty. And he wanted to find out why.

He'd just assumed Emery's killer was a man. But he shouldn't have done that, not when he knew so many strong, capable women.

"What are you up to, Mother?" he asked. His jaw ached from how hard he clenched it to hang on to his smile.

Maisy peered up at him fearfully, as if she heard the anger he was fighting so hard to hide. He didn't want to scare his daughter, even though fear had his heart pounding fast and hard.

Why hadn't he considered his mother a suspect before? She was the one his father had hurt the most when he'd changed his will to exclude her. She was the one in most need of money and maybe even revenge—if she blamed Cole for that will change like the rest of his family.

"I'm playing with my granddaughter," she told him. Her smile appeared to be as forced as his.

They had never been particularly close, not like he and his father. Not like he was with his grandfather. He'd already realized he reminded her too much of his father, and she'd hated Coleman. Could she hate her own son, too?

Enough to try to kill Shawna? To try to kill him? Those shots had struck the house pretty close to where he'd been standing. Whoever had fired them must have intended to hit him.

"What are you up to?" she asked him.

"What do you mean?"

"At first I bought your performance in the dining room, just like Shawna did." She shook her head. "But now that I've had a chance to think about it…" She glanced down at the little girl she held on her lap.

If she hadn't been holding his daughter, he would have confronted her already, would have demanded she tell him where Shawna was. She must know. According to Manny, she'd helped Shawna shake him from his protection duty. Why? Had Tiffani done something to her? Had she hurt her?

His mother shook her head again. "I'm not buying it."

"What?" he asked.

"Your act," she said. "You love her. You always have. You always will. Just like your father loved Natalie."

His mother had known about Natalie. And he hadn't. Maybe his parents had been closer than he realized. Or maybe his mother had found out another way. She was smart and resourceful.

Smart and resourceful enough to be a killer?

Maisy's blue eyes widened as she stared up at him. "Who do you love, Daddy?"

"Your mommy," Tiffani answered.

The little girl's brow puckered with confusion. "But then why won't you marry her?"

His mother arched a blond brow and asked, "Yes, why won't you?"

"You know why," he said, and he glared at her.

She sighed. "I think I do know why. Shawna has no idea, though."

He had wanted it that way—when he'd put his plan in motion. But now he was second-guessing himself. He hadn't expected Shawna to ditch Manny and run off somewhere by herself. He'd thought he would find her here in the garden with Maisy and Nikki.

Nikki was there, but she'd let his mother close, had let her cuddle the little girl. Too close, if Tiffani was the threat. Nikki must have begun to have her suspicions, too—she moved her hand to her holster.

Cole shook his head. He didn't want his mother shot. Despite their difficult relationship, he loved her and didn't want her hurt. Maybe he could talk her down. "Where is she, Mother?" he asked.

"Who?" she asked innocently—and his mother had never been innocent. She'd been conniving and resourceful and determined. And drunk. She must have started drinking again. That had to be why she'd been so emotional the past couple of days. Was she drunk now?

"Shawna," he said, and the anger began to seep into his voice. "Where is she?"

"I don't know."

Maisy must have seen the concern on his face because she began to tremble in her grandmother's embrace. "Where's Mommy?" she asked.

Cole shook his head. "*I* don't know."

The little girl turned to Tiffani and asked, "Grandma, where's Mommy?"

His mother sighed and replied, "She needed a little time to herself."

"She can't have a little time to herself right now," Cole said. Not when she was in danger. The last time she'd gone out for air, Manny had been knocked out and she'd nearly been killed.

Unless his plan had worked. If it had, she might not be in any danger. But his mother had already gotten wise to him. The killer, if it wasn't her, might have, as well.

Cooper and Manny were right. It was a stupid plan.

"Where is she?" he asked again.

His mother shrugged. "I really have no idea. You know her better than anyone, Cole."

For the first time, he realized it was true. He had

always known Shawna better than anyone else in his life or hers. He'd spent the past six years thinking he must have been wrong about her or she wouldn't have married another man. But he understood now why she had.

For Maisy. To protect Maisy.

And he intended to do the same. He held out his arms to the little girl. She hesitated for just a moment before she wound her arms around his neck, so he could lift her from his mother's lap. He clasped her close to his madly pounding heart.

Then he looked down at his mother and noticed the hurt flash through her eyes. She felt rejected again, just as his father had continually rejected her. Why had she stayed? Had she loved Cole, or had she loved the money?

Either way he felt bad for her. Hopefully she had real love now with Jeff. But she didn't seem happy. In fact, since the funeral, Tiffani had been more upset than he'd ever seen her. His eyes narrowed as he re-membered her running from the library—from the urn.

"Mom," he began.

She jumped up from the garden bench. "I don't know where she is," she said.

But that wasn't the question he'd been about to ask her. She didn't give him the chance to ask anything else as she took off.

"Grandma's upset," Maisy said.

"Yes, she is," he agreed. "Did she visit very often at your old house?"

The little girl nodded.

Were she and Shawna friends? Or had Tiffani, like everyone else, suspected that Maisy was her grand-daughter?

"Did she visit you or Mommy?" he asked. She had worked with Shawna, helping to coach the cheer-leaders at the same high school where Emery Little had taught band.

"Daddy." The little girl's face flushed. "I mean my old daddy. She visited him a lot."

Things were beginning to fall into place for Cole. But Maisy was too young to understand, and she shouldn't have to. He lifted her chin with his finger and stared into her eyes. "He was your daddy, and he always will be."

Emery Little had protected Shawna and Maisy. And no matter what else had been going on with the man, he hadn't deserved to die.

"What about you?" she asked. "Don't you want to be my daddy?"

"I do," he told her. "Very much."

"Daddy married Mommy, so he could be my daddy," Maisy said. "But you don't want to marry Mommy."

Cole glanced at Nikki. "Was she near the din-ing room earlier?" Had she overheard how he'd lied?

Nikki shook her head. "No. She picked up on that this morning."

"Why do you think that?" he asked the little girl.

"Because you're mad at Mommy."

He was. He wanted to be. Oh, hell…

But knowing why Shawna had done what she

did—for their daughter—he couldn't be mad at her. He assured Maisy, "No, I'm not."

"Are you mad at me?" she asked, and her soft voice cracked with emotion.

He shook his head vehemently. "Of course not. I think you're the most amazing little girl, and I'm so thrilled you're my daughter. I very much want to be your father."

Nikki—tough bodyguard who never cried— blinked furiously at the tears welling in her eyes. When she caught him looking, she covered her eyes and said, "Must be a stray eyelash or something."

Maisy called his attention back to her when she asked, "What about Mommy?"

"We'll find her," he promised.

She shook her head. "What about Mommy?" she asked again. "Do you love her? Do you want to be with her?"

He'd just made a big production of lying to his entire family about his feelings for Shawna. But he couldn't lie to his daughter.

"Can you keep a secret?" he asked.

She gave him a solemn nod, although he suspected she wasn't even as good at keeping secrets as Manny. It didn't matter. He would find another way to protect Shawna because his plan had been idiotic. He wasn't protecting her when he was the one actually hurting her.

"I love your mommy very much," he said. "I always have and I always will."

The little girl's face lit up. "So you are going to

marry her!" She tightened her grasp around his neck and hugged him close.

And like Nikki, he was suddenly blinking hard. He wanted to make Maisy happy. But that wasn't the only reason he wanted to marry Shawna. He wanted to make her happy, too. But he couldn't do that if he couldn't find her.

He had to find her. And she had to be safe—for all their sakes.

Shawna waited out on the second-floor balcony until they changed guards outside Xavier's room. Once the two men moved down the hallway to talk, she quickly moved from the balcony into his room. She didn't want to be seen. She wanted time to think. But first, she needed to vent.

"How could you?" she asked him.

"What?" Xavier blinked hard as if trying to focus on her. Had he been sleeping? Or had he been poisoned again? Maybe she wasn't the only one who'd slipped into the room while the guards were changing.

She rushed to the bed. "Are you all right?"

He nodded. "Yes, of course I am." He scooted up against the headboard. "I just need to get out of this bed. It's making me feel like an invalid."

"You're not," she said. He was one of the strongest men she knew—physically and mentally. "You should be able to get up today."

He swung his legs over the bed to do just that, but she put her hand on his shoulder. "But you need to stay away from the cigars."

"I'm cured," he promised. "I no longer have any desire for them."

"Yes," she agreed, "when something causes you pain, you shouldn't want anything to do with it anymore."

He groaned. But she knew he wasn't hurting. "That's why you're mad. You found out about the will."

"How could you?" she asked again.

"You and Cole belong together," he insisted.

She'd once thought that, too. But not anymore. She shook her head. "If that were true, he wouldn't have broken our engagement."

"You haven't figured out yet why he did that?" he asked, as if he knew.

"He told me why," she said. That she was too dependent, too clingy—that she was a damsel in distress always in need of rescuing. "And he hasn't changed his mind," she said. "He just announced to your entire family that he won't ever marry me, no matter what. He doesn't want your money. And most important—" her voice cracked as pain jabbed her heart "—he doesn't want me."

Xavier must not have heard the emotional break in her voice that echoed the one in her heart. He began to laugh. Heartily.

"What's wrong with you?" she asked. Maybe he wasn't as mentally strong as she'd thought he was. Was he getting dementia? Was that why he'd done the things he had? Changing his will? Hiring Cole to be her bodyguard?

"I'm laughing because he's such a hypocrite," he said. "He condemns me for the things I've done, and he's every bit as manipulative as I am."

"Manipulative?" she asked. That was the last thing she'd think of when it came to Cole. "What are you talking about?"

"You two have known each other most of your childhood and nearly all of your adult lives," he said. "And you can't figure out why he's done what he has?"

She had begun to suspect that he might have been trying to protect her. Six years ago. But now? She shook her head even as hope burgeoned inside her.

"So you think he just all of a sudden fell out of love with you?" Xavier asked. "Or what, that he was playing you all along with the declarations of never-ending love he'd professed to you since grade school? With the ring he gave you from an inheritance he only touched for you?" He snorted. "That was some acting, I guess, to cover up the fact that he's just a creep who was using you."

She gasped.

"I guess Cole is just a bad man then," his grandfather said. It was clear he didn't believe it.

And neither did Shawna.

"No, he isn't," Shawna automatically defended him. Despite everything, Cole was a good man. He was a hero. He was brave and protective…

The suspicions she'd begun having clicked into place, and she knew, without a doubt, what he'd done six years ago. And what he was doing just now…

He was protecting her.

She wanted to rush to him and profess her love. But because he'd gone to such great lengths to protect her, she couldn't foil his plan. Like Xavier, the killer might not have bought it either.

She shouldn't have had Cole's mother help her get rid of Manny. Of course there was at least one guard outside this door. She was safe because Xavier was safe. She needed to make sure that Cole knew she was safe, too. He was probably incredibly worried and upset with Manny and with his mother. She needed to get word to him right away.

But when she opened the door, it wasn't a guard standing outside it. Cole's stepfather stood there, and he had a curious expression on his face.

Usually he seemed happy and harmless. But the look on his face now had goose bumps rising on Shawna's arms.

"Excuse me," she said as she tried to maneuver around him. But he clasped her arm tightly in his hand, pinching her flesh.

"You and I can either go back in the old bastard's room and finish this up with both of you," he said, "or we can step out onto the balcony."

She drew in a deep gulp. If she went back into Xavier's room, Jeff would kill them both. If she went onto the balcony with him, she might have a chance to escape. But as he pulled her through the balcony door, she remembered how high up they were—with the brick patio beneath.

If she jumped...

She was certain to get hurt.

But she knew Jeff intended to do more than hurt her as she turned and stared into the barrel of a gun. "Why?" she asked.

He had seemed like such a nice man—so mild mannered, like Emery. Why would he resort to murder? She shuddered, realizing he was the one; he'd set the bomb that had killed her husband, her friend.

"Is all of this just about the money?" she asked. She knew money motivated most people, especially Cole's family. But she couldn't understand it pushing someone to murder. She didn't want to die just for money. She didn't want to die at all. She loved her daughter too much to leave her. And she loved Cole, too.

She had to figure out a way to disarm this killer before he killed again.

A sense of peace washed over Jeffrey. There was no way now—no way for Cole to thwart his plan. First, he would kill Shawna, then he would kill that cagey old bastard. Then it wouldn't matter that Xavier had changed his will.

Hell, it didn't matter now.

"No," he replied. "This isn't about money."

"What's it about then?" Shawna asked.

"Love."

Her brow furrowed. "I don't understand."

"Of course you don't!" he exclaimed. "The only one who might is Cole…" He sighed. "He loves you. But you never really loved him."

"That's not true," she protested.

"You married another man," he reminded her. "You kept his child from him. And after all that pain you caused him, he's still trying to protect you."

She glanced around as if Cole had appeared. But Jeff would make sure Cole didn't rescue her this time. Not that he would hurt him—because that would hurt Tiffani.

He hadn't realized until recently that she actually loved her son. So it was good that he'd missed Cole when he'd shot at him, although he'd regretted not ending it then. But now that he knew she loved the boy, he couldn't kill him. That would only bring Tiffani more pain. And he didn't want to do that. Not really.

He was only trying to prove his love for her. Why didn't she understand that?

Why had she never seen just how much he loved her?

This would prove it; he would get her the inheritance she'd been denied when Coleman had died. A smile curved his lips as he thought of that.

Killing Coleman Bentler had been immensely satisfying. During the AA meetings where they'd met, Tiffani had talked about her husband, about how he'd killed a woman and gone unpunished just because he was rich. She'd known the woman. Natalie Montoya had been her idol and mentor on the beauty pageant circuit. That was why Tiffani had sought out the man who'd killed her. She'd wanted to punish him.

Instead Coleman had punished her. He had deserved to die for killing Natalie and for hurting Tiffani.

Killing Shawna wouldn't feel quite as satisfying. Unlike Coleman Bentler, she had done nothing to deserve death. But still she had to die, so that Tiffani could get the money she'd wanted for so long. So she could get the happiness she deserved.

And maybe, when she realized what lengths Jeff had gone to in order to make her happy, she would love him like he loved her. And if she didn't...

If she couldn't...

Then he didn't care to live without her love anymore.

Chapter 23

Cole should have realized right away where Shawna would go—to Xavier. She was probably as furious with him for his manipulations as Cole was. It wasn't as if she actually wanted to marry him. She had just lost her husband, after all.

But had Emery Little ever really been her husband? Cole had questions about that relationship. He had a lot of questions for Shawna. But first he had to find her.

He hurried toward the wing of the house where his grandfather's bedroom was. But as he turned the corner in the hall, he saw a body slumped against the wall. Blood spattered the brocade wallpaper over Lars's head and soaked into his hair, turning the pale blond a rusty red.

His hand on his gun, Cole rushed forward, but the hallway was empty except for Lars. He leaned down and felt for a pulse, and he breathed a ragged sigh of relief when he found one. Lars was alive, but he needed help.

He probably wasn't the only one. Cole jumped up and hurried around the corner and pushed open the door to Xavier's room. The old man gasped and pressed a hand to his heart.

"What the hell's going on?" Xavier demanded. "You nearly scared me into having another heart attack."

"Are you alone?" Cole asked. He glanced around the expansive master suite. The blankets were tossed back on the bed, and the old man had dressed.

"Yes," his grandfather replied. "Shawna just left, though."

Panic gripped Cole, pressing so hard on his chest he could barely draw a breath. "When?"

"Just a couple of minutes ago," Xavier said. "You didn't see her in the hallway?"

No. And he should have, if she'd gone into the hall. "Did you hear anyone outside the door?" Cole asked.

Xavier shook his head, and the color began to drain from his face. "What's wrong? What's happened?"

Cole tossed his cell phone at his grandfather. "Call Cooper for help. Someone knocked out Lars in the hall and must have taken Shawna."

The old man's hand trembled as he grabbed the phone and began to scroll through the contacts. But when Cole opened his door again, his grandfather stopped and called out, "Wait! Don't go off alone."

"I can't wait," Cole said and closed the door between them. He might already be too late.

Right outside the door was a sitting area and on the other side of the sitting area was a door to the second-story balcony. Even before he noticed the shadow beyond the drapes, he knew that was where they were. Shawna and the killer.

Cole moved quickly and quietly toward the door. He carefully turned the handle and popped it open just enough that he could hear.

"I—I don't understand why you're doing this," Shawna murmured, her voice quavering with fear, "if it's not about the money."

"I told you," the man said, his voice sharp with frustration and anger and madness. Cole barely recognized that it was his stepfather talking—his stepfather holding a gun on the woman Cole loved. "It's about love."

"How can murder ever be about love?" Shawna asked.

"She doesn't know—she doesn't appreciate how much I love her," Jeff said. "How I'll do anything to make sure she gets what she deserves."

"So it is about the money," Shawna insisted. "It's about her not inheriting Coleman's estate, so you're going after Xavier's."

Jeff snorted. "I didn't kill Coleman Bentler just so she would inherit his money. I killed him to free her from that murdering bastard."

"What?" The question slipped unbidden through Cole's lips.

Jeff whirled toward him with the gun, firing wildly. Cole ducked, and a bullet splintered the jamb just above his head. Another bullet shattered the glass in the balcony door.

Shawna's scream shattered the quiet afternoon, making Jeff whirl back toward her. But before he could fire again, Cole fired.

He had to make sure his bullets didn't stray and strike Shawna on the other side of his stepfather. He had to make sure Jeff didn't get the chance to squeeze the trigger of his gun again and kill the woman Cole loved, whom he had always loved.

He couldn't lose Shawna forever.

He fired quickly but carefully. Gunshots echoed after his, and he knew Jeff had fired. The man staggered and fell—right on top of Shawna who'd dropped to the floor of the balcony.

And Cole feared he hadn't acted fast enough. That he hadn't been accurate enough.

That he had lost her.

Shawna wiped the blood from her face. It wasn't hers. Like Cole, she'd ducked just in time to avoid getting her head blown off. Jeff had not been so lucky. She shuddered as she remembered the horror of that moment, of Cole taking a life to save hers.

"Are you okay?" he asked her.

He'd picked her up and carried her away from the balcony, away from Jeff's body. She was in the bathroom off her bedroom now, cleaning up.

"I didn't get hit," she assured him. Again. That had been his first concern when he'd pulled Jeff's body off her.

His gaze met hers in the mirror. "That's not what I'm talking about."

She sighed. "That wasn't the worst thing I've seen." That had been the explosion.

Cole must have remembered she'd witnessed that because he apologized.

"Why would he kill Emery? Why would he hurt anyone?" she asked. "I still don't understand."

She might never know the reason. Jeff might have taken them to his grave.

"I know," a soft voice murmured.

Shawna and Cole turned to see his mother, who stood in the bathroom doorway. For the first time since Shawna had met her, the woman looked her age. Deep lines marred her forehead and her face, with dark circles rimming her eyes.

"Are you all right?" Tiffani asked her.

Shawna nodded and asked, "Are you?" The woman had just lost her husband at the hands of her son. Would she be okay?

"I'm sorry," Tiffani replied, looking at both of them.

"Were you part of it?" Cole asked, his voice gruff with emotion. "Did you put him up to all of this?"

His mother gasped with shock and pain. "Of course not. I had no idea."

"He killed my father," Cole said. "I didn't even think you knew Jeff yet when that happened."

"I didn't," she murmured. "Not really. I'd only seen him a few times in our AA meetings."

"The meetings," Cole murmured. "I remember that was where you'd met him."

"I wasn't there to meet anyone," Tiffani said. "I knew I needed to quit drinking and get strong enough to leave your father."

Shawna couldn't blame her. The man had never treated her well.

"But you didn't leave," Cole said. "So Jeff took care of my father for you."

"I didn't know," she said. "I just thought he was driving too fast—like always."

"Like he had the night Natalie died," Cole said.

"Natalie?" Shawna asked the question then.

"The woman Cole's father loved and lost in high school," Tiffani said.

Cole was staring at his mother with his eyes narrowed with suspicion. "How did you know about her? He never mentioned her to me."

She laughed bitterly. "He never mentioned her to me either. I knew her." She uttered a wistful sigh. "I idolized her. She was so beautiful. So sweet. She didn't deserve to die. And he wasn't charged with anything for killing her."

"Is that why you did it?" Cole asked. "Why you got pregnant? To punish him?" He looked queasy, as if the thought of being a punishment was sickening.

It was. Shawna squeezed his arm in sympathy.

"I realize now that he was punishing himself," Tiffani said. "That was why he worked so hard. Not for the success or the money. He did it out of guilt.

I set out to punish him and actually wound up feeling sorry for him at the end." Tears filled her eyes again, but she blinked them back. "All these years I thought he'd driven off that cliff on purpose. I had no idea Jeff..."

Cole still looked suspicious. "You really had no idea what Jeff was up to? That he was a killer?"

She shivered and shook her head. "I still can't believe it."

Shawna couldn't either and he had nearly killed her more than once.

"He was so sweet to me," Tiffani told her son. "After how your father treated me, I appreciated the way Jeff lavished attention on me. He loved me."

"That's why he did it," Shawna said. "That's what he said... It was because he loved you."

She shook her head. "I tried to tell him that I didn't need the money. I didn't need anything but love."

"But not his love," Cole said. "You loved someone else."

She nodded. Then she turned toward Shawna. But she couldn't meet her gaze. And Shawna knew.

Suddenly she knew who her friend had loved and thought he could never have—until recently—until he'd gotten hopeful again. "Emery?"

Tiffani nodded. "I loved him so much...but I couldn't hurt Jeff. He worshiped me. I couldn't treat him the way Coleman had treated me. So Emery and I, we sneaked around."

Cole looked from one to the other of them, as if he expected to see jealousy or resentment. Shawna smiled and slipped her arms around the other woman, pulling her close. "He loved you—so much."

"I don't understand," Cole said. "Why did he marry you then?"

"He was my friend," Shawna said. "He was only ever my friend." She remembered that she'd been the one to introduce him to the woman she'd thought would one day be her mother-in-law. That had been before Cole had broken their engagement and her heart.

Tiffani pulled out of Shawna's embrace. "I couldn't believe he was really interested in me. He was so much younger—so good-looking." Coleman had obviously destroyed her self-esteem. That must have been why she'd married Jeff. She'd felt secure with him.

And instead she'd married a killer.

"He loved you," Shawna assured her again.

"I know," Tiffani agreed, and emotion cracked her voice. "I finally accepted that. I was going to leave Jeff. I told him that I didn't love him like he deserved to be loved. But he didn't understand. He kept thinking he had to prove his love."

Cole cursed. "That's why he did all of this."

His mother nodded. "I'm so sorry," she murmured again before she ran from the room.

Cole stared after her. "I should go," he said. "I should talk to her—make sure she's okay."

Shawna nodded in agreement even though she didn't want him to leave her. She needed to feel his arms around her, needed to hear that what he'd told his family had just been part of a plan to protect her.

But she didn't stop him. She just watched him leave. She couldn't help but wonder if he would come back. His assignment was over now. She no longer needed protection. But she still needed him.

She wished she'd told him so. But maybe he had been telling the truth when he made that announcement to his family. Maybe he would never be able to forgive her for marrying another man and for keeping his daughter from him.

Like Emery, she might never get her chance at her happily ever after.

Cooper was damn glad this assignment was over, although his client seemed to be struggling with accepting that fact.

"The case is closed," he told Xavier. "The police closed it, too." They'd just left the house after taking reports from everyone involved. The coroner had taken away Jeffrey Inman's body. "There is no longer any threat."

He doubted Cole's mom had any involvement in her husband's misdeeds. She'd been too distraught. But her husband apparently wasn't the man she was mourning.

What a mess.

And he'd thought his family was colorful. The Paynes had nothing on the Bentlers. No wonder Cole hadn't wanted anything to do with this bunch.

Maybe that was why Xavier pleaded with Cooper, "Stay on just a little while longer."

Cooper shook his head. He wanted to get back to his family. He had never appreciated them more.

"I'll make it worth your while," Xavier said as he pulled out his checkbook.

He had just written a sizable one. Cooper didn't need or want another. "My brother's team has already left for the airport."

Parker had another assignment for them, one the new chief of the River City Police Department had personally asked him to handle. The chief was also their new stepfather, so Parker was doubly anxious to get his team back to tackle the job.

"And my team's packing to leave," Cooper went on. "You don't need a bodyguard any longer."

Xavier snorted derisively. "You've met my family, right? You don't think Jeffrey Inman was really the only one who wants me dead?"

"I don't think any of your other relatives have plans to off you right now," Cooper said. But he wasn't one hundred percent confident.

"You never know with this bunch," Xavier said. "I could use at least one bodyguard for around-the-clock protection."

Cooper grinned. "And do you have any particular bodyguard in mind for this assignment?"

Xavier grinned, as well. "Well, I think your sister is kind of cute."

Nikki was a little busy at the moment; she and Dane had taken Lars to the hospital for a CT scan. Once he'd regained consciousness, he'd insisted he was fine, but Nikki had wanted to make certain.

"Her fiancé might take exception to that," Cooper warned him.

Xavier expelled a regretful sigh. "That's too bad."

"We both know she's not the bodyguard you really want to stick around," Cooper said.

Xavier sighed again.

"I understand what you're trying to do here," Cooper said. "That you want your grandson back—"

"You've met the rest of my family," Xavier said again. "He and Shawna and their little girl… They're the family I want with me."

Pity for the old man overwhelmed Cooper. Despite all his money, Xavier Bentler couldn't buy what he really wanted. Family. Cooper felt a flash of guilt for all the years he'd taken his own family for granted. As a Marine, he'd spent so many years away from them. He wanted to get home more than ever now.

But he couldn't leave in good conscience without warning the old timer. "I'm sorry, sir. I can't give you what you want. And I'm not sure Cole will either. He's made a home for himself in River City. He has a career that I think he enjoys and he has friends who are like family to him. I don't think you'll be able to get him to stay here."

"Not even for Shawna and his daughter?"

Now Cooper was concerned. Cole obviously didn't need the job.

Was he about to lose one of his best employees and friends?

Chapter 24

He'd made a hell of a mess of things with Shawna. Twice. It was his fault she'd married Emery. At least according to his mother.

But Tiffani only knew what Emery had told her. He could have lied to spare her feelings. Cole hoped that he'd told the truth, that he'd been as honest and good a man as everyone believed him to be.

Cole was still in the den where he'd found his mother beside the urn of Emery Little's ashes. He stared at it as if searching for answers. He wished now that he hadn't blown off the man when he'd tried to talk to him.

What had Emery wanted to tell him? The same things he'd told Cole's mom about his relationship with Shawna? Cole would never know. But he could get the answers he sought from Shawna if she would talk to him.

She'd looked so devastated when she ran out of the dining room earlier that day. He'd wanted her re-action to look genuine, but he should have found a way to protect her that wouldn't have hurt her—six years ago and now. Maybe he wasn't as good a pro-tector as he'd thought he was—as the medals of valor the Corps had awarded him had led him to believe.

But he was a good bodyguard. Even before he heard footsteps against the hardwood floor, he sensed the person's presence. It had always been that way with Shawna, though. His body was so connected to hers that it reacted whenever she was close; his pulse began to beat faster, his blood heated and his skin tingled.

She must have known that he would know she was there because she softly asked, "Do you think I should give her the urn?"

"Do you think that's what he would have wanted?" he asked in return.

"He loved her."

"You know that?"

"I didn't know she was the one," she said. "But I knew he was in love with someone."

"And you married him anyway?"

"He couldn't be with her," she said. "I didn't know why." She sighed. "I didn't even know the love of his life was a woman. I had no idea what the situation was." Her voice cracked. "I should have been a bet-ter friend to him."

"He was protecting her," Cole surmised. So Emery

Little really had been a good guy. "Just like I was trying to protect you."

"When?" she asked.

"Six years ago," he admitted. "That was why I
broke our engagement. I didn't think I was going to
make it back from that mission. And I didn't want you
to mourn me like you'd mourned for your parents."

She'd been so devastated after losing them, and
he'd felt so helpless to comfort her. Of course, he'd
just been a kid then.

Her breath caught. "How was that protecting me?"

"I figured it would be easier for you if, when I
died, you hated me," he explained.

Tears glistened in her dark eyes. "I did," she murmured. "I did hate you for breaking up with me. For
breaking my heart. But I still mourned you."

"I didn't die." He'd almost wished he had. Then
his plan would have made sense. Breaking up with
her would have been the right thing to do. But he saw
now how wrong he had been, how horribly wrong.

"I mourned the boy I loved," she said. "I mourned
the man who would have never hurt me because it
seemed like *he* had died."

Cole flinched. He had always promised that he
would never hurt her, that he would always take care
of her.

"When you joined the Marines, I was warned that
you might change," she said. "That you might not be
the man I'd fallen in love with when you came back.
I hadn't believed that was possible...until that day."

Cole's heart broke with regret. He had been so
wrong. He could not have been more wrong.

"But then you came to the funeral and I saw you with your friends and with your grandfather and…" her voice cracked again "…with our daughter. And I saw that man—the good man—who I thought would never hurt me."

That was probably why she had made love with him. He'd thought she'd been scared and vulnerable and he'd felt guilty for taking advantage of her.

"I wish I could tell you that I am that man," Cole said. "But I'm not. Whoever told you that I would change was right."

"Your mother…" she said. "She said that the things you would see, the things you would have to do would change you."

Like Natalie dying in that car crash had changed his father. It wasn't quite the same. But it was close.

"I did a lot, saw a lot," he conceded. "And it did change me. It taught me to know what really matters."

She nodded as if she understood. He knew that she didn't, that she couldn't. She hadn't been where he'd been, hadn't done what he'd done. And he was grateful for that. But she'd been through some of her own tragedies recently.

"You matter," he said. "That never changed. I did what I did six years ago to protect you. And you still matter, that's why I did what I did in the dining room today. I was trying again to protect you."

She stared at him, her dark eyes wide. She'd washed off his stepfather's blood, but he could see it yet, could see how she'd looked. He remembered how he'd thought for just a minute that a bullet had struck her despite his attempt to save her.

He didn't need her to say it. He said it for her. "I failed. I failed you twice. So I can understand if you don't want to give me another chance."

"Chance?" Her brow furrowed with confusion.

"When I talked to my mother, she gave me something," he said. "Something you gave her six years ago."

All the color drained from her face. "She was supposed to give that back to you."

He pulled the ring from his pocket and held it out to her. "It never should have left your finger," he said. "I was a fool to break our engagement." And her heart. He'd been such an idiot. Could she forgive him?

She stared at him, and that ring, as if she were horrified to see it again. If she hated it, hated the bad memories associated with it, he would buy her another. Hell, he'd buy her anything she wanted.

"Please, Shawna, give me another chance," he implored her. "Give us another chance."

She pressed her hand over her mouth as if holding back a cry, then turned and ran from the room with no answer.

But then, after what he'd done to her—twice—he didn't deserve one. He didn't deserve another chance.

Shawna closed her bedroom door and leaned against it, her heart beating wildly. She shouldn't have run. But she'd never been as afraid as she'd been when Cole had proposed for the second time. Not even when Jeff had held that gun on her. Or when the bomb had exploded...

Cole's proposal terrified her in a way that she'd

never been afraid before. It shook her to her core—
she'd wanted to accept. She'd wanted to throw her
arms around his neck and hang on so tightly that he
would never leave her again.

And that terrified her.

She'd been devastated when he broke up with her
before. She didn't want to go through that again. She
worried that he would leave her again because she
wasn't convinced that he loved her.

Knuckles brushed softly against the door at her
back. A deep voice called out, "Shawna…"

He'd followed her. She hadn't been certain that
he would, and she'd needed a moment to calm her
wildly pounding heart. But before she could lock the
door and send him away, the knob turned, and the
door opened.

"Are you all right?" he asked her. He didn't look
like he was; his handsome face was tense, his jaw
clenched, his blue eyes dark with concern.

Before she could answer him, he said, "Of course
you're not all right. You've been through so much
this past week. And I—I was an idiot to ask you for
another chance."

"Why did you ask me?" she asked.

"Because I want you to marry me," he said. "I
want us to be a family for Maisy."

She flinched. "So you're doing this for Maisy."

"Shawna—"

Anger swept her pain aside, and she lashed out at
him. "Why would you do that to her?"

"Do what?" he asked, his brow furrowed with confusion. "Give her a family? A father and a mother?"

"Give her the life you lived, with a husband resenting his wife for getting pregnant?" she asked.

"That's why you didn't tell me when you found out you were pregnant?" he asked. "You thought I would act like my father did...that I would treat you like he treated her. With contempt."

She nodded. She wouldn't have been able to bear his resentment. His mother was a far stronger woman than she was. But then Tiffani hadn't loved Cole's father, not like Shawna loved Cole.

His resentment would destroy her.

"This situation is entirely different," he said. "My father and mother never loved each other. I loved you."

"Loved?" That was why she'd run away—because she was afraid his love was only in the past. How could she expect him to still love her after what she'd done? After she'd married another man and kept his child from him?

He stepped closer, his arms reaching for her. "Shawna—"

She pressed her hands against his chest, holding him back. "I understand," she told him as emotion rushed up, choking her. "You feel betrayed... because I married Emery...because I didn't tell you about Maisy..." He couldn't trust her any more than she could trust him. Maybe they'd just hurt each other too much to recover what they'd once had.

Cole said nothing, and his arms dropped back to his sides.

"We can't build a marriage on mistrust and resentment," she told him.

"I don't resent or mistrust you," he said. "But it's clear that you do me."

"I'm not sure why you want to marry me," she said. "If it's just for Maisy."

He shook his head. "No."

"Then why?"

"Because I love you," he said.

"You loved me," she reminded him of his words.

"I never stopped," he said. "Sure, I was hurt when you married another man so quickly—"

She stepped forward and pressed her fingers over his lips. "I didn't love Emery," she said, "not like I loved you."

He flinched at her use of the past tense.

But she continued, "He and I never had a real marriage. We were only ever friends. There was nothing romantic between us. Nothing passionate. He married me only to help me protect Maisy."

And maybe to be close to Cole's mother. Shawna hoped he'd gotten something out of their arrangement because he'd given everything for it. His life.

"He helped protect her from my family," Cole murmured. "That's why you didn't want anyone to know she's my child."

She nodded. "I've seen how they treated you. And I didn't want her to go through any of that. I didn't want her to be involved with them at all." She sighed. "But I couldn't sever all ties—not with your grandfather or your mother. We were all there for each other when you left for boot camp and through your deployments."

"I know that was hard for you," he said. "That's

why, as my missions got more and more dangerous, that I thought it would be better for you if we broke up. Then you wouldn't care if I was in danger or if I didn't return at all."

She drew in a shaky breath at the thought. "I would have cared."

"I know it was a bad idea," he said. "And I don't know if I can ever forgive myself for hurting you. So I understand that you can't forgive me either."

She stared into his eyes, and she saw the regret he felt. And she saw even more than that; she saw the love. The same love she felt for him. Never-ending…

No matter how long they'd known each other or what they'd been through, they would always love each other.

"Yes," she said.

He flinched as if she'd struck him and pulled back. "I'm sorry," he said. "I won't bother you anymore." He turned toward the door.

"No," she said. "That's not what I meant. I can forgive you. I already have." Because she understood why he'd done what he had.

He turned back, but he looked as though he was holding his breath. His body was tense, his jaw rigid. "You have?" he asked. "Why?"

"Because I love you," she said. "I've always loved you."

He arched a brow as if doubting her.

She smiled and conceded, "Even when I hated you, I loved you. And I love you still."

"I love you," he said. "That's the only reason I

proposed. Because I want to spend the rest of my life trying to make up for hurting you."

"You already have," she said. "You gave me Maisy, who is my life. And then you saved my life—a few times."

He shook his head. "You're no damsel in distress, Shawna Rolfe. You would have saved yourself if I wasn't here."

She wasn't so certain about that. But she smiled and admitted, "I am tougher than I realized."

And maybe she would have never realized that if he hadn't broken up with her, if she hadn't spent the past six years essentially on her own. Emery had been her friend, but he'd never been her mate, the way Cole had been her soul mate.

"You were always tough," he assured her. "You experienced a lot of loss at a young age, and you survived it. I didn't want to put you through that again, but I should have realized that you could handle it, if you'd had to. That you could handle anything."

He was right. She could. Even though his current job as bodyguard put him in danger, she could handle that. She was tough. Tough enough to risk her heart on a man who'd already broken it once.

And smart enough to know that he would never willfully break it again.

Rising up on tiptoe, she wound her arms around his neck and pulled his head down to hers. She kissed him, nibbling at his lips until he parted them. Then she slid her tongue inside his mouth.

He groaned.

She giggled as a sense of power rushed through

her. She'd forgotten how she used to be able to affect him. When she'd thought he no longer loved her, she'd lost that power. But now she knew he loved her—that he had always loved her.

She flicked her tongue over his bottom lip, teasing him as she pulled back. Then she skimmed her lips over the slight stubble on his cheek to the edge of his jaw, and she nibbled again. As she kissed her way down his throat, she unbuttoned his shirt and skimmed her hands over his chest, over the sculpted muscles.

He was perfect, so damn perfect. She had never wanted him more than she did now.

When she trailed her fingers over his washboard abs to the buckle of his belt, he sucked in a deep breath. When she skimmed her fingers over the erection straining against the fly of his jeans, he expelled a ragged sigh.

And his control snapped. He pushed her hand aside to strip off his own clothes. Then he stripped off hers, pulling her shirt over her head and pushing down her pants. He lifted her from the pile of their clothes and laid her on the bed.

She reached out and closed her fingers around his erection, stroking her palm up and down the length of him.

"Shawna," he said between gritted teeth. "You're driving me crazy."

"Good," she said with a smile. She loved being able to affect him the way he affected her. She loved him.

He narrowed his eyes, then he returned the favor,

kissing and caressing her into madness. She squirmed against the mattress as his mouth moved over her body. He nibbled at her breasts, gently tugging at each nipple before moving farther down her body.

He'd barely flicked his tongue across her core before she came, crying out his name. She clasped his shoulders and tugged, pulling him up. Then she pushed him onto his back and she straddled him. He clenched her hips in his hands and lifted her so that he could ease inside her.

She arched and thrust and finally he filled her as only he could. On top, she set the rhythm, and she set it slow, teasing them both.

"Shawna…" He uttered her name on a groan. The cords in his neck and his shoulders strained as he struggled to regain control.

She leaned forward and kissed his neck and his chest. He cupped her breasts and stroked his thumbs over her nipples. The sensation shot to her core, which pulsed and throbbed with the need for release. She increased the rhythm to a frenzy, and he moved his hands to her hips again, helping her move as fast as he thrust.

"Yes, yes," she told him as she began to peak. Finally the tension broke, and an orgasm overwhelmed her. He swallowed her cry of pleasure with his mouth as he kissed her. Then his body tensed and shuddered as he found his own release.

Panting for breath, she collapsed onto his chest. He stroked his hand over her back, which was slick with sweat. Then he cupped the back of her head in his palm, like he always did.

"So what were you saying yes to?" he asked. He turned them both onto their sides so they faced each other on the tangled sheets.

"When?" she asked coyly and peered up at him through her lashes. "I think I just said yes a few times."

He grinned. But then his tone turned serious as he said, "Before I nearly walked out of here, you said yes. I thought you were saying yes that you could never forgive me. But that wasn't it at all. What was it?"

She smiled. "Ask me again."

His blue eyes brightened with hope and with love. He rolled out of the bed and knelt beside it. And after fishing something from the pocket of his jeans, he asked, "Will you make me the happiest man alive and marry me?"

"Yes," she said.

He slid the ring on her finger. It fit a little more snugly than it had the first time he'd proposed. But she'd been younger then; she hadn't had a child yet, his child. "Is it too tight?" he asked anxiously.

She shook her head. "No. It fits perfectly. I won't need to take it off again anyway." Because they both knew, there was no way they were breaking this engagement. They loved each other too much to ever be apart again.

He breathed a sigh of relief. "I was so worried that you wouldn't be able to forgive me."

"I worried about the same," she admitted.

"You have no reason to worry," he assured her. "I will do anything to make you happy. Are you sure you want this ring? I can buy you another—one that has only happy memories attached to it."

She stared down at the big diamond and shook her head. She would never forget how he had initially proposed to her with this ring—on the playground where they'd met, where he'd saved her the first time. "The happy memories are all I remember," she assured him. "I don't want another ring. I just want you."

He was all she had ever needed—until he'd given her their daughter. Now she had more than she'd ever expected from life. She had everything.

"I'll even quit the Payne Protection Agency and move back here if you want," he offered.

She gasped in horror more than relief. "Absolutely not." She hadn't asked for proof, but he'd just given it—he really loved her if he was willing to sacrifice so much for her. Too much. "You love your job and you love your friends. Maisy and I will move to River City."

He grinned wider than she'd ever seen him. "You'll love it," he promised her. "The Payne family is amazing. You'll be embraced and accepted and appreciated."

She knew that he'd found in the Paynes the family he'd always wanted. She couldn't wait to meet all of them.

"What about my grandfather?" he asked. "You didn't want to leave him."

"We won't," she said. "We'll bring him with us."

Cole snorted. "How will we get him to move?"

She smiled. "We'll use his weapon against him. Manipulation."

"You'll manipulate him?"

"Not me," she said.

And she knew the old man wouldn't stand a chance.

Nikki studied her fiancé's face. His skin was pale, even paler than his sister Emilia's translucent skin. His pale blond hair had been washed but still had a faint reddish tinge from the blood that had stained it. He'd needed stitches.

"I'm sorry," she murmured to him as they sat side by side in the back of the small private plane.

He turned toward her. "You're sorry?" he asked. "You were right. I needed stitches and I do have a concussion." He flinched as he said it, as if his own voice was about to shatter his skull.

"I'm sorry for what I put you through all the time, with me being a bodyguard," she said. "Now I know what it feels like to worry."

He squeezed her hand and offered her his endearing lopsided grin. "You're not changing jobs, though," he told her. "And neither am I. It's okay that we worry about each other." He gestured at Dane sitting in the front of the cockpit with Manny who was flying the plane. "It's what we all put each other through. It doesn't change how we feel about each other or our jobs."

She squeezed his hand back. "No, it just makes us appreciate each other more," she agreed. "It makes me want to get married even sooner."

Lars touched his head. "Man, I must have gotten hit harder than I thought. I think you just said you don't want to wait to get married."

"I don't," she said, then she leaned forward and spoke to Manny in the cockpit. "Can you reroute this flight to Vegas?"

Lars gasped. "Vegas?"

She nodded. "I can't wait to be your wife." No one was more shocked than she was to hear those words coming out of her mouth. She'd vowed once to never get married—despite or maybe because her mother, the wedding planner, had probably had Nikki's wedding planned since the day she was born.

Manny turned back toward them, which had Dane anxiously gripping the dash. "Hey, watch where you're going!" the nervous flyer protested.

Manny chuckled. "We're fine. I have eyes in the back of my head."

"So use those eyes to look at Nikki and Lars," Dane advised him.

Manny turned back toward the windshield, but then he had to shout his question to them. "You really want me to put this down in Vegas?"

Lars, with his sexy half grin, turned toward Nikki. And regret slammed through her. "Do you really want to do this?" he asked.

"Marry you? Absolutely," she said. But she couldn't deny her mother those plans, not when the woman had sacrificed so much for all of them. Always. She sighed.

Lars's grin widened as he squeezed her hand again. "We have all the time in the world to get married," he assured her. "Nothing's going to happen to either one of us. You're too tough and my head is like a cement block."

A giggle slipped through her lips. Damn Lars. He was the only man who ever made her do something ridiculously girly—like giggle and feel like more of a woman than she'd ever felt. "True," she agreed. Loving him only made her tougher. "We'll be fine."

"So no Vegas," Manny said.

"No." They would go home to River City and wait for the elaborate wedding Nikki's mother had planned for her for so many years.

"You're thinking about Cole now," Lars said, as attuned to her as ever.

"Do you think he'll come back to River City?" she asked.

Dane whirled around in his seat. "You think he'd stay here?"

"He's not leaving Shawna again," Manny said.

"But will she take him back?" Dane asked.

Nikki nodded. "Yes, she will. But I'm not sure she can leave the life she built here. I'm not sure she can leave Xavier."

"She won't," Lars agreed.

So they could lose their friend. He might quit the agency and move back home. Except he'd said the Bentler mansion had never been home for him.

Nikki knew, though, that home wasn't a place; it was a person. Cole had two people now: Shawna and Maisy. With his grandfather, he actually had three.

Nikki worried that they as a team were about to lose their person. She squeezed Lars's hand, knowing how much it would bother him after everything his unit had endured together.

He grinned again, but it was obviously forced. He was worried, too.

"We left a man behind," Manny murmured.

It would bother him the most if they lost Cole. The two of them were the closest, even shared an apartment. Manny's life was changing now, too.

Nikki couldn't help but think that this assignment had changed them all. Nothing would ever be the same.

Epilogue

Church bells pealed out, announcing that the wedding was about to begin. It was time. Cole caught Manny's arm before he could leave the groom's dressing room. "Hey," he said. "Let me fix your tie." His fingers shook a little as he fumbled with the black bow. It didn't have to be perfect—he knew that.

But Lars's and Dane's ties were crisp and straight, like Cooper's. Cole had no idea what his looked like. Thankfully Manny hadn't tied it for him. Xavier had, his fingers steady and nimble despite his age. But Manny was Cole's best man, so he wanted him to look nice.

And maybe he needed just another minute...

"Nervous?" Manny asked him, then he held his

breath as if dealing with some nerves of his own. Or maybe Cole had pulled the tie too tight.

Cole shook his head and clarified, "Anxious." He was eager and excited to begin his new life with his new family.

Manny's tie was as straight as it was going to get, so Cole turned and headed for the door. He and his groomsmen walked to the front of the church to stand before the altar. He stayed next to the minister while each of his guys took turns walking halfway down the aisle, with its white runner, to meet a bridesmaid and escort her to the front.

Shawna hadn't been in River City long, but just as he'd known she would, she'd fallen in love with the city and especially with the people. His friends were now her friends and family as well, so she'd included all the women in her wedding party.

Cooper escorted his gorgeous blonde wife Tanya to the front; Dane escorted the ethereal Emilia; Lars, Nikki; and Manny escorted his supermodel fiancée, Teddie. While she was beautiful, Teddie was very down to earth, so much so that she and Shawna had instantly become best friends.

Cole smiled as he watched Manny escort the red-haired beauty toward the front. Manny's dream girl was soon to become his wife. He'd pushed back his wedding plans and so had Lars and Dane in order to let Cole have the first opening at Penny Payne Lynch's white wedding chapel. They all knew, like he did, that this wedding was six years overdue.

Manny and Teddie reluctantly parted at the front. As Manny stepped behind him, he squeezed Cole's shoulder. He couldn't have been a better friend or best man.

But Cole was about to marry his best friend. He focused on the back of the church, but the next person down the aisle wasn't the bride. She wore a small white dress though and was a perfect miniature of her perfect mother.

Maisy skipped down the aisle, scattering rose petals from the basket she carried. Before she took her place on the bride's side of the aisle, she hurled herself at Cole. He caught her up in his arms and swung her around, and he felt pure joy.

She was so special, this little girl, this little piece of him mixed in with so much Shawna. She kissed his cheek before murmuring, "Put me down, Daddy. Mommy's about to come down the aisle."

Everyone chuckled as Cole did as he was told. They knew how he was totally twisted around his daughter's little finger. He didn't mind, though. He loved it—because he loved her so much. Maisy skipped the couple of steps across the aisle to slip her hand into Teddie's and lean against her. Just as her mother had become fast friends with the former supermodel, the little girl had fallen for her, too, and vice versa. Teddie was like an aunt to her.

The music stopped for a dramatic pause before it changed to the bridal march. Cole returned his focus to the back of the church where Shawna stood at the end of the white runner, her hand on Xavier's arm. It was only appropriate that the old man give away the bride since he'd been so instrumental in reuniting them.

To repay the favor, Cole had had Nikki help him track down the woman Xavier claimed was the love of his life. Fortunately, Edith was still alive and as active and vibrant and sharp as Xavier. Much to Xavier's relief, she had never blamed him for her husband's death. She had also never remarried. She sat now in the front pew, waiting for him to join her.

Despite his age, he walked quickly. Maybe he was anxious to join Edith. Maybe he was anxious to bring Shawna to the altar—to Cole.

As they neared him, Cole focused only on her. A wispy veil covered her face but only for a couple more seconds. After she and Xavier stopped in front of him, the old man lifted her veil and kissed her cheek.

Then the minister asked, "Who gives this woman to be married to this man?"

Three voices replied. Xavier, Shawna and Maisy said in perfect unison, "We do."

Everyone laughed. But Cole blinked back tears. It meant a lot that Shawna could give herself to him after how he'd hurt her. But all that pain was in their past. As for their future... It was beyond happy.

Xavier had moved to River City, as well. He hadn't been able to tell Maisy no when she'd sweetly asked him. Cole wasn't the only one twisted around her little finger. Fortunately, she was too much like her mother—too pure of heart to ever become spoiled like Cole's uncles and cousins.

Maisy wasn't the only one the old man was trying to spoil, though. Xavier had already given Cole and Shawna a wedding present—of a vast estate. The house was so big that there was plenty of room for him to live with them. There was so much property that Cole had already convinced Manny and Teddie to build a house on it, as well. He was pretty sure that Lars and Dane would build their homes there, too.

His family—his real family—would always be close to him. Xavier had left the rest of his family in California to fight over the house and the company. At the moment, Tiffani was in charge of the business. He predicted that was unlikely to change; she was tougher than he'd realized. She was also here for the wedding, sitting in the front row on the other side of Edith.

When Xavier went to sit with them, Cole, unwilling to wait for the end of the ceremony, stepped forward and pressed his lips to Shawna's. She looked so beautiful in her lace gown with her black hair swept up on top of her head.

"Daddy," Maisy called out in a loud whisper. "You're supposed to wait till the end to kiss Mommy."

But he'd already waited too long for his best friend—his soul mate—to become his wife. He kissed her again before stepping back.

He was flustered, like Shawna, but they made it through the ceremony. And at the end, when they were pronounced husband and wife, they turned and ran hand in hand from the church—ready and anxious to start spending the rest of their lives together.

* * * * *

SPECIAL EXCERPT FROM

H HARLEQUIN®

ROMANTIC suspense

*When Liz James is threatened and her daughter
kidnapped, she turns to Harley Maxwell for support.
Fortunately, he's an undercover cop who, for sixteen
years, has been tracking the man who kidnapped her
daughter. Will Harley's quest for revenge overshadow
his chance at love with Liz?*

*Read on for a sneak preview of the next book
in the Undercover Justice miniseries,*
Undercover Passion *by Melinda Di Lorenzo.*

Liz asked, "Can I really trust you, Harley?"

He felt his eyebrows knit together in puzzlement. "Trust
me? With the gun? It's a legal licensed firearm. And I'm
fully trained. But if you're not comfortable…"

"No. That's not what I mean. I'm sure that you wouldn't
do something reckless."

"I definitely wouldn't. So what do you mean?"

"I mean if I tell you about what happened today, can you
promise not to go to the police?"

The question made him want to roll out his shoulders to
relieve a sudden kink. If she was about to confess to some
involvement with Garibaldi, he wasn't sure he wanted to
hear it.

*Because you already decided she was innocent based on
the feel of her lips?*

He shoved off the self-directed question and went back to
work on her leg, cleaning it more thoroughly this time than
he had on top of the roof. "That's a tough question to just
give a yes or no to."

"Is it?" she sounded almost disappointed.

And he had to admit that he felt something similar. With her tempting lips and all, he really didn't want her to be on the wrong side. It was the only small positive that he thought had come out of the current sequence of events. Knowing that her store was under fire had led Harley to infer that she couldn't be involved with Garibaldi. The possibility that whatever crime had been committed at Liz's Lovely Things was a third party seemed unlikely.

But not impossible.

He chose his next words carefully. "I think of myself as a decent guy, Liz. One who does the right thing whenever possible. So as far as trust is concerned…you can count on me for that, every time."

"And if it's not a black-and-white situation?" she asked softly, opening her eyes and directing a clear, serious look his way.

He met her gaze. "I think a lot of things fall somewhere in the gray spectrum, actually. You have to sort through it to figure out what's right and what's wrong. But doing things that could result in people getting hurt…that's a hard limit for me. I wouldn't ever endanger Teegan, or ask you to do anything that might. The cops are the good guys."

She bit her lip, looking like she was trying to hold back tears. Harley couldn't help himself.

Garibaldi be damned.

He pushed up and reached out to fold her into an embrace.

Don't miss
Undercover Passion *by Melinda Di Lorenzo,*
available November 2018 wherever
Harlequin® Romantic Suspense books and ebooks are sold.

www.Harlequin.com

Need an adrenaline rush from nail-biting tales
(and irresistible males)?

Check out **Harlequin Intrigue®**
and **Harlequin® Romantic Suspense** books!

New books available every month!

CONNECT WITH US AT:

Facebook.com/groups/HarlequinConnection

 Facebook.com/HarlequinBooks

Twitter.com/HarlequinBooks

 Instagram.com/HarlequinBooks

Pinterest.com/HarlequinBooks

ReaderService.com

 **HARLEQUIN®**

**ROMANCE WHEN
YOU NEED IT**

SGENRE2018